A HOUSE NOT MEANT TO STAND

"Tennessee Williams' last play, *A House Not Meant To Stand*, reminds me of those last great shocking paintings that Philip Guston produced in the 1970s: grotesque hilarious cartoon figures driving around junkyards in jalopies with overblown tires, dressed in KKK sheets and boots, leaving only putrefaction behind. Williams, who could always hear America's heart before the rest of us, tapped into the same zeitgeist: a world where the Kowalskis rule, where the Blanches and Almas and Lauras and Hannahs have long since given up the slightest hint of a dream, where they (and we) are truly trapped with the brutes. And the surprise: *A House Not Meant to Stand* is a ferocious scalding comedy. Tennessee Williams pushed the boundaries right up to the very end."

—John Guare

BY TENNESSEE WILLIAMS

PLAYS

Baby Doll & Tiger Tail

Camino Real

Candles to the Sun

Cat on a Hot Tin Roof

Clothes for a Summer Hotel

Fugitive Kind

A House Not Meant to Stand

The Glass Menagerie

A Lovely Sunday for Creve Coeur

Mister Paradise and Other One-Act Plays:
These Are the Stairs You Got to Watch, Mister Paradise, The Palooka, Escape, Why Do You Smoke So Much, Lily?, Summer At The Lake, The Big Game, The Pink Bedroom, The Fat Man's Wife, Thank You Kind Spirit, The Municipal Abattoir, Adam and Eve on a Ferry, And Tell Sad Stories of The Deaths of Queens...

Not About Nightingales

The Notebook of Trigorin

Something Cloudy, Something Clear

Spring Storm

Stairs to the Roof

Stopped Rocking and Other Screen Plays:
All Gaul is Divided, The Loss of a Teardrop Diamond, One Arm, Stopped Rocking

A Streetcar Named Desire

Sweet Bird of Youth

The Traveling Companion and Other Plays:
The Chalky White Substance, The Day on Which a Man Dies, A Cavalier for Milady, The Pronoun 'I', The Remarkable Rooming-House of Mme. Le Monde, Kirche Küche Kinder, Green Eyes, The Parade, The One Exception, Sunburst, Will Mr. Merriwether Return from Memphis?, The Traveling Companion

27 Wagons Full of Cotton and Other Plays:
27 Wagons Full of Cotton, The Purification, The Lady of Larkspur Lotion, The Last of My Solid Gold Watches, Portrait of a Madonna, Auto-Da-Fé, Lord Byron's Love Letter, The Strangest Kind of Romance, The Long Goodbye, Hello From Bertha, This Property is Condemned, Talk to Me Like the Rain and Let Me Listen, Something Unspoken

The Two-Character Play

Vieux Carré

THE THEATRE OF TENNESSEE WILLIAMS

The Theatre of Tennessee Williams, Volume I:
Battle of Angels, A Streetcar Named Desire, The Glass Menagerie

The Theatre of Tennessee Williams, Volume II:
The Eccentricities of a Nightingale, Summer and Smoke, The Rose Tattoo, Camino Real

The Theatre of Tennessee Williams, Volume III:
Cat on a Hot Tin Roof, Orpheus Descending, Suddenly Last Summer

The Theatre of Tennessee Williams, Volume IV:
Sweet Bird of Youth, Period of Adjustment, The Night of the Iguana

The Theatre of Tennessee Williams, Volume V:
The Milk Train Doesn't Stop Here Anymore, Kingdom of Earth (The Seven Descents of Myrtle), Small Craft Warnings, The Two-Character Play

The Theatre of Tennessee Williams, Volume VI:
27 Wagons Full of Cotton and Other Short Plays
includes all the plays from the individual volume of *27 Wagons Full of Cotton and Other Plays* plus *The Unsatisfactory Supper, Steps Must be Gentle, The Demolition Downtown*

The Theatre of Tennessee Williams, Volume VII:
In the Bar of a Tokyo Hotel and Other Plays
In the Bar of a Tokyo Hotel, I Rise in Flames, Cried the Phoenix, The Mutilated, I Can't Imagine Tomorrow, Confessional, The Frosted Glass Coffin, The Gnädiges Fräulein, A Perfect Analysis Given by a Parrot, Lifeboat Drill, Now the Cats with Jeweled Claws, This is the Peaceable Kingdom

The Theatre of Tennessee Williams, Volume VIII:
Vieux Carré, A Lovely Sunday for Creve Coeur, Clothes for a Summer Hotel, The Red Devil Battery Sign

POETRY

Collected Poems

In the Winter of Cities

PROSE

Collected Stories

Hard Candy and Other Stories

One Arm and Other Stories

Memoirs

The Roman Spring of Mrs. Stone

The Selected Letters of Tennessee Williams, Volume I

The Selected Letters of Tennessee Williams, Volume II

Where I Live: Selected Essays

A PARTIAL VIEW OF THE STAGE SET FOR THE ORIGINAL GOODMAN THEATRE PRODUCTION
DESIGNED BY KAREN SCHULZ

TENNESSEE WILLIAMS

A HOUSE NOT MEANT TO STAND

A GOTHIC COMEDY

FOREWORD BY
GREGORY MOSHER

EDITED, WITH AN INTRODUCTION, BY
THOMAS KEITH

A NEW DIRECTIONS BOOK

A House Not Meant to Stand is published by special arrangement with The University of the South, Sewanee, Tennessee.

Cover and front matter design by Rodrigo Corral.
Text design by Sylvia Frezzolini Severance.
Frontispiece photo by Karen Schulz Gropman
Manufactured in the United States of America
New Directions Books are printed on acid-free paper.
First published as New Directions Paperbook 1105 in 2008
Published simultaneously in Canada by Penguin Canada Books, Ltd.

Library of Congress Cataloging-in-Publication Data:

Williams, Tennessee, 1911–1983.
A house not meant to stand : a gothic comedy / Tennessee Williams ; foreword by Gregory Mosher ; edited with an introduction by Thomas Keith.
p;. cm.
"A New Directions Book."
Includes bibliographical references.
ISBN 978-0-8112-1709-5 (alk. paper)
I. Mosher, Gregory. II. Keith, Thomas. III. Title.
PS3545.I5365H68 2008
813'.54—dc22 2007049511

New Directions Books are published for James Laughlin
by New Directions Publishing Corporation
80 Eighth Avenue, New York, New York 10011

CONTENTS

Foreword ix

Introduction xiii

Production Credits 1

A House Not Meant to Stand 3

Sources, Notes, and Acknowledgments 89

FOREWORD

Tennessee Williams's one-act play *Some Problems for the Moose Lodge* premiered in 1980 at the Goodman Theatre, while I was its artistic director. I had not sought it out; it wouldn't have occurred to me then that you could call Tennessee Williams to see if he had a new play. In fact, when Gary Tucker, a fixture in the then-nascent Chicago theater scene, rang me up to ask if I'd like to meet America's most famous living playwright, I assumed it was a practical joke of some sort. But when I arrived at the Pump Room, I spotted the man himself, seated at one end of a wide banquette. I took the remaining place setting, on the other end, while Gary held forth from the middle. I could barely hear Williams, and perhaps this is why, as we ate our fish, the three of us said the same things over and over. Gary: "Tom has a new play, and you have to do it." Me: "We'd be honored." TW: "Perhaps Mr. Mosher would like to read the play before deciding." Me: "We'd be honored to do the play, Mr. Williams." Gary: "You have to do Tom's new play." And so forth.

Not long thereafter this brief comedy opened as part of an all-

Williams evening called *Tennessee Laughs*. After one performance, the playwright Richard Nelson mentioned that *Moose Lodge* seemed less like a complete one-act than the beginning of something longer. I shared the comment with Williams, the one-acts played out their run, and we all, I thought, moved on to other matters. But a few months later a full-length play, bearing the title *A House Not Meant to Stand*, arrived in the mail. We reassembled the cast, went back into rehearsal, and opened in the spring of 1981, again with Tucker directing, and again in the 135-seat Goodman Studio Theatre, where David Mamet's *Glengarry Glen Ross* and David Rabe's *Hurlyburly* would later premiere. Near the end of this run, Williams said he'd like to continue working on the play, and asked me if the Goodman could produce yet another version, with a new director, in the larger theater. We agreed, of course, and incorporated Williams' rewrites into a final incarnation, which premiered in April 1982 under the direction of André Ernotte.

Twenty-six years later, the play has been published by Tennessee's beloved New Directions. This delay, and the fact that a fine play by America's finest dramatist has never had a major follow-on production, are among the strange and sad phenomena of the American theater. *A House Not Meant to Stand*'s absence from the stage might be attributed to Williams' executrix, the Lady Maria St. Just, who missed the productions, didn't like what she read, and effectively embargoed it. But then again, nobody was beating down Maria's door, and she was hardly alone in skipping the trip to Chicago. For the last few decades of the writer's life, the consensus was nearly unanimous: Williams was best enjoyed in revivals of the early masterpieces. When it came to new work, the one-time life of the party was no longer on the guest list.

So by 1980, when he arrived in Chicago, where *The Glass Menagerie* had opened thirty-six years earlier, he was in a tough spot. His *Clothes for a Summer Hotel* had closed earlier that year after a Broadway run of only fourteen performances, and Williams knew this meant he would no longer be able to attract the collaborators and great gobs of cash necessary to do a play there. The man who signed his letters "En avant!" was not, however, inclined to quit. Williams' endurance embarrassed many people, including some of those who loved him most. But in a champion's waning years, the spectator's discomfiture is, finally, beside the point. The writer, like the prize-fighter, must choose when—or whether—to withdraw. He is the one who runs the lonely pre-dawn miles, and whose blood streams so publicly.

As he reworked, over nearly two years, the script that would become *A House Not Meant to Stand*, his confidence grew, and with good reason. Replacing a tone of haunting grace with one of gothic savagery, he summoned echoes of *The Glass Menagerie*, bringing the absent Mr. Wingfield down from his photo as a grinning, tempestuous monster, and transmogrifying a mother's dreams of gentleman callers into hallucinations of missing children. Best of all, he gave this nightmare a distinctive comic force. But as Williams gradually rediscovered his voice, the esthetic and emotional stakes rose precipitously.

When it started to seem that he might just vanquish the nay-sayers by writing his best play in a good long while, the pressure he felt was nearly intolerable. So I was not surprised to look up from my desk, shortly after we began rehearsals for the play's third version, to see a very agitated writer standing in the doorway. I invited him to sit, but he declined, and announced that he was leaving for his Key West house. I said I was deeply sorry to hear it, not least because the actors would miss him. He told me he doubted that, because he was withdrawing the play. I pointed out that we had a contract. He started to yell, arriving with astonishing velocity at a lyric I knew to be a Golden Oldie on the Tennessee label: "You are my enemy!" This was an obvious untruth, meant only to provoke, and easy to ignore. But as he stood, robed in his fur coat, more exhausted than exalted in his ferocity, waiting for my response, I suddenly realized his distress must be mixed with wearisome *déjà vu*. I thought of the colleagues, far more significant than I, who had played this scene with him over the decades, and I was moved beyond measure. Like an ill-prepared understudy, but wanting to be worthy of him, I approached. He regarded my extended arm, the aspect of which was clearly conciliatory, and stepped back. "I don't like to be *touched* by my enemies." He turned to leave, and though I followed him through the backstage corridors, out the front door, and to a waiting car, I found him to be past persuasion. His extended retreat to warmer climes—he did not return to Chicago until the final previews—deprived the actors of an invaluable perspective, not to mention the bracing geniality of his comradeship. Both the production and the script were no doubt diminished by his absence. But one can ask only so much. Williams displayed more than enough courage simply by entrusting his script to people he hardly knew, depending one last time on the kindness of strangers.

The morning after opening night, I went to his hotel to say goodbye and get him to the airport. He was ensconced in the President's Suite, but because some new VIP was arriving, we had sworn a solemn oath to relinquish it by 9 A.M. I was relieved to find the bags packed. But the playwright was at his desk, a cup of coffee next to his portable typewriter. The reviews—mixed but encouraging and respectful—were spread out in front of him. He was smiling as he typed. I watched for several moments. "Tennessee. . ." I said quietly, "we have to go." He barely looked up. "Not now, baby, I'm *working*."

Outside the hotel, we promised to see each other soon in New York, or Key West, or even New Orleans, where he had once shown me the haunts of his fabled life. Time, the longest distance between two places, passed. We had dinner or a drink a few times, and talked of future work. Then suddenly, nine months later, he died, in New York, in the Sunset Suite of the Hotel Elysée.

Tennessee Williams was a brave writer, and he gave the American drama, with all due respect to Mr. O'Neill, its bravest body of work. His plays—and the remarkable film versions they engendered—reflected and shaped American culture to a degree unmatched by almost any other American writer, let alone playwright. As you read this play, I think you'll be glad that he wrote to the very end.

Gregory Mosher

January 2008

INTRODUCTION: A MISSISSIPPI FUNHOUSE

"I am offering you my *Spook Sonata* and probably it would astonish Strindberg as much as it does you and me."

—Tennessee Williams, from draft notes for
A House Not Meant to Stand, A Gothic Comedy

Aristophanes, Shakespeare, Molière, Sheridan, Wilde, Shaw, Kaufman and Hart, Kanin, and Coward wrote comedies. Simon, Feiffer, McNally, Durang, Rudnick, and Ayckbourn write comedies. Did Tennessee Williams write comedies? What is "a comedy" by Tennessee Williams, anyway? Is it like an absurd, satiric, cruel, black, regional or ridiculous comedy by Ionesco, Albee, Orton, Guare, Shepard, Henley or Ludlam? Well . . . not quite.

Of all Williams' full-length plays only five, maybe six, are generally considered to be comedies: *The Rose Tattoo*, *Period of Adjustment*, *Will Mr. Merriwether Return from Memphis?*, *A Lovely Sunday for Creve Coeur*, *A House Not Meant to Stand*, and, maybe, just maybe, *Kingdom of Earth*. Of these, *The Rose Tattoo* is the only one commonly understood to be a romantic comedy, and two others the author qualified with subtitles—*Period of Adjustment, or High Point Over a Cavern, A Serious Comedy*, and *A House Not Meant to Stand, A Gothic Comedy*. These two plays both take place at Christmastime in imminently collapsing houses and feature two couples, a history of mental health problems, a dog, and a visit from the police—apparently requisite components for comedy.

One reason Williams' comedies are more difficult to categorize as such is because they are a lot like his dramas. When Williams put two unlikely one-acts—the disturbing *The Mutilated* and the equally bleak but especially hilarious, *The Gnädiges Fräulein*—together in 1966 for an evening off-Broadway he titled *The Slapstick Tragedy*, neither the collective title, nor the plays themselves was a success with the critics or with the public. Any demarcation line within a Williams play that might define it as a comedy is rather fluid—drama and comedy emerge simultaneously from the author's experience, imagination and subconscious. In this Williams has something in common with Chekhov and Beckett—his humor springs from the futile, lost, violent or desperate lives of the characters. And should you find them funny, well, then, perhaps a nerve has been touched. There are numerous accounts of how during performances of his plays, Williams was liable to suddenly cackle wildly at a serious moment while others in the audience sat confused, wondering what was so funny or who the madman was at the back of the house.

If one's introduction to Williams is *reading* his plays, one would not necessarily appreciate the humor played out by Stanley Kowalski and Blanche DuBois, for example, upon their initial meeting in scene one of *A Streetcar Named Desire*. Once a dramatic tone is established, the humor may be overlooked, but it's there:

> STANLEY: My clothes're stickin' to me. Do you mind if I make myself comfortable? [*He starts to remove his shirt.*]
>
> BLANCHE: Please, please do.
>
> STANLEY: Be comfortable is my motto.
>
> BLANCHE: It's mine, too. It's hard to stay looking fresh. I haven't washed or even powdered my face and—here you are!

On the page the drama dominates, but performance can reveal Williams' wit, earthiness and comic rhythms. In much of his later work, from the 1960s and 1970s, the humor becomes broad—slapstick, grotesque, the Grand Guignol—and even reads like comedy. Williams was just as prolific in the last twenty-four years of his life as he had been in the previous twenty four: in the forty-eight years from 1935 to 1983 he completed at least thirty-three full-length plays and at least seventy one-acts. Williams had no way of knowing that his last fully-realized play would be full-length, that in it he would return to his Mississippi roots, that it would be a comedy, or that it would premiere in Chicago nine months before his death.

Tennessee Williams' connection to Chicago is profound—*The Glass Menagerie*, produced there in December of 1944 and *A House Not Meant to Stand* produced there in May of 1982, turned out to be the bookends of his long career in the professional theater. The analogy is imperfect: *Battle of Angels* closed after the first week of its out-of-town Boston tryout in 1940, and a work in progress called *Gideon's Point* was performed at the Williamstown Theater Festival in August of 1982. However, the thematic connections between the *The Glass Menagerie* and *A House Not Meant to Stand,* and the importance of their productions to Williams' artistic life, are striking.

When *The Glass Menagerie* opened in the middle of a blizzard, critics Claudia Cassidy and Ashton Stevens, along with several other local reviewers and columnists, pushed, wrote, cajoled, and rallied the public until audiences grew large enough to sustain the production for a transfer to Broadway, where the play brought Williams success of an enormity he had not fully expected. In her first review of *The Glass Menagerie*, Cassidy wrote that the play "holds in its shadowed fragility the stamina of success. If it is your play, as it is mine, it reaches out tentacles, first tentative, then gripping, and you are caught in its spell." With *Menagerie*, Williams opened the door to a new kind of American theater in which common speech reached lyric heights and realism was present only when necessary, and he put a dysfunctional (as it would now be understood) American family under a microscope. And no matter how tender the beauty or tensile the fever of this play, the sense that at its nucleus it was and is Williams' own story can never be avoided.

Claudia Cassidy was also present when the final version of *A House Not Meant to Stand* opened in the spring of 1982, and reviewed the play on WFMT radio. Fully aware of the author's triumphs and misfortunes over his four-decade career, Cassidy found herself witness to a much darker creation. Referring to Williams' use of the word "Gothic" to describe his play, Cassidy said:

> "If we take the term in the sense of the mysterious, the grotesque, and the desolate, then *A House Not Meant to Stand* is a gothic structure, and Southern gothic at that. But it is Tennessee Williams' Southern gothic and it is shrewd as well as bitter, often sharply, acridly funny as well as sad . . .a rotting house . . .as on the edge of an abyss, a kind of metaphor for the human condition inside. . . . [The play] is indeed mysterious, grotesque and desolate but whoever said that theater is none of those things? There is here the acute compassion Tennessee Williams has always had for the victims of the world we live in."

Williams subtitle, *A Gothic Comedy*, is significant, as is the reference in his stage directions to Strindberg's *The Spook Sonata* (as the title is sometimes translated, or *The Ghost Sonata,* as it is commonly known). By the end of *The Ghost Sonata*, a young student realizes not only that many members of the Stockholm family he has been visiting are dead, but that they are all, including himself, in a kind of hell. Most of the members of the Pascagoula, Mississippi family are alive, but Cornelius and Bella McCorkle are dying, their house is crumbling around them and their children are deceased, or hospitalized, or perpetually unemployed. The McCorkle's refer to the disposition of people as "living remains"—theirs is a house haunted by its living inhabitants and their pasts. Bella is so attuned to her grief that apparitions appear to her—she hears the sounds of children playing, representations of her offspring from a past that may well have been for her as idyllic and full of love as she remembers it. These specters and supernatural voices are not spooks in the way Strindberg would have used them, nor are they like Williams' ghosts in *Clothes for a Summer Hotel* and *Will Mr. Merriwether Return from Memphis?* They do not belong to the total world of the play, only to Bella's world—they are Bella's means to find release from her sorrow.

A comedy? Well it begins with rhythm, and the rhythms of this comedy are peculiar. No matter how slow, decrepit, or traumatized they may be, the characters in this play rarely seem to stop moving. There is an overarching sweep that involves dozens of entrances and exits for Bella and her son, Charlie, and most of the characters are engaged in a persistent sitting and standing, coming and going, pausing and starting, that continues to the final moments of the play, but is rarely swift. While *A House Not Meant to Stand* is not a farce, its rhythms of are almost those of a farce in slow motion. Perhaps it would be helpful, if not entirely accurate, to call it a "Mississippi farce." The dialogue is not paced for fast laughs, but ambles with intermittent jolts of energy, often spoken directly to the audience. Cornelius confides in the audience, looks to them for moral support, or turns to them in frustration as when Charlie finds his father's plan to run for Congress laughable and Cornelius shouts suddenly at the audience, "WAR! IMPERIALIST AGGRESSION AND YOU KNOW IT, THAT'S RIGHT, ALL OF YOU KNOW IT!—SUCKERS . . ." Four times, twice in each act, the action shifts to a higher gear: when Emerson is taken away, when Bella runs out of the house and onto the highway, when Stacey speaks in tongues, and when the police take Cornelius and Charlie away in a squad car. The transitions are often abrupt and complement the stream-of-consciousness madness in the house.

A comedy. Williams let his fear of madness run rampant through these characters. Cornelius wants to have Bella committed because she is "gone in the head," but even as she functions in a haze between the past and the present—trying to secure the Dancie money for her children Charlie and Joanie—she has moments of dazzling clarity. When Bella outfoxes Cornelius' attempt to confront her about the location of the hidden Dancie money, she is positively skillful. Emerson, likewise declared mentally unstable by his spouse, Jessie, seems rational enough: "There's too much putting away of old and worn out people. Death will do it for all. So why take premature action?" And yet, Emerson's compulsive sexual fixation, ignited when he meets Charlie's sexy and fantastically pregnant fiancée, causes him to shake uncontrollably. The scene in which "the men in the white coats" take Emerson away is breathlessly cruel, and shows a malevolent streak in Cornelius.

During the time Williams began writing the earliest version of this play, the one-act *Some Problems for the Moose Lodge*, a new conservative movement, later misnamed "The Moral Majority," was becoming vocal in America. In response, politicians from Carter to Bush, Sr. declared themselves "born-again." Williams' choice to make Stacey what he calls "a born-again Christian," and one of the most outrageous characters in the play may have been his not so subtle comment on this faith-on-the-sleeve trend in public life. Stacey's "holy-roller" fit in the second act is a riotous kind of madness, yet the appellation of born-again Christian is a misnomer; as Stacey speaks in tongues and rolls on the floor she acts out a parody of a Pentecostal. Stacey, the outsider, is sensitive to the viciousness in the McCorkle house. Despite the dogma associated with her faith, she displays genuine empathy for the late Chips, going so far as to fondly describe gay men she has known—an annoyance to Cornelius and a comfort to Bella.

A comedy. Williams' notes, drafts and many revisions on *House* during 1980, 1981, and 1982 reveal his search for a core theme. A master of play titles, Williams' prospective titles for *House* offer clues to how his thinking evolved. The title of the original one-act, *Some Problems for the Moose Lodge,* was plainly chosen for comic effect. In the next draft, *The Dancie Money*, Williams shifted his focus by introducing Cornelius' interest in Bella's moonshine inheritance. *Our Lady of Pascagoola* embodies both Williams' vision of Bella's boundless love as well as her comic potential. Other titles—*The Legendary Bequest of* [*a*] *Moonshine Dancer*, *Laundry Hung on the Moon*, and *For Tatters of a Mortal Dress*—also position Bella as the central figure of the play. Cornelius dominates the prospective titles, *Being Addressed by a Fool*, *A House Not Meant to Last Longer than the Owner*, and *What Odds are Offered by the Greek in Vegas?*, which reflect his fear of mortality and his ambitions, financial and political. Still other draft titles—*The Disposition of the Remains*, *Terrible Details (A Gothic Comedy)* and *Putting Them Away*—contemplate the sad lives of the McCorkle children. *The Disposition of the Remains* (a double entendre on the disposition of "living" remains), places the focus on Cornelius' indifference and Bella's agony regarding Chips' death. *Putting Them Away* and *The Terrible Details* can refer to both Chip's interment and Joanie's confinement in a mental ward, and could also suggest the threat of institutionalization to Emerson and Bella. Williams chose *A House Not Meant to Stand* for the title of the second Goodman production and did not change it again. Not such a funny title.

*

Parallels are frequently drawn between Williams' characters and the population of his own life—sometimes explicitly intended by the playwright as in his frankly autobiographical works *Vieux Carré* and *Something Cloudy, Something Clear*. Keeping in mind the shades of Tennessee Williams' father found in Big Daddy from *Cat on a Hot Tin Roof*, Boss Finley from *Sweet Bird of Youth*, and Charlie Colton from *The Last of My Solid Gold Watches*, there has never been another character like Cornelius in the Williams canon who so clearly stands for Williams' own father, also named Cornelius. Aspects of Williams' brother Dakin are also present in Cornelius—pointedly, his failed aspirations for political office.

The three McCorkle children, a gay son, a straight son, and a mentally disturbed daughter, can be easily equated with Tom, Dakin and Rose Williams. Bella and Cornelius McCorkle are a natural parallel to Williams' parents, Edwina and Cornelius—a married couple perpetually at war. But more curiously in Cornelius and Bella McCorkle and in Emerson and Jessie Sykes one can find Williams himself. It seems he found a repository in *A House Not Meant to Stand* for his fears about illness and death, for his frustrations with growing old, and possibly for some of his failures and his follies. Williams' experiences as he aged are evident in each of these characters: Cornelius' aggression toward his family and deep sense of failure; Bella's weight and health troubles and her desperate need to recover love lost; Emerson's betrayal by his wife and his best friend; Jessie's fixation with youth and sex. By the late 1970s Williams had the osteoarthritis Cornelius complains of, his heart and weight problems, not to mention his smoking and drinking, and he got along with a daily battery of pills, including Cornelius' cotazyme and Donnatal. Cornelius, Emerson and Bella spill enough bottles of pills on the stage to create a potential hazard for the actors. In *A House Not Meant to Stand* Williams was able to integrate his overwhelming feelings about aging and health in a way audiences might empathize with, or at least share a laugh about.

When Cornelius McCorkle responds to a description of his dead gay son Chips as "the handsomest boy at Pascagoula High" by saying he was actually "the prettiest girl at Pascagoula High," it is a potent connection to the real Cornelius Williams. It may have satisfied Williams to put that scorn on stage to garner a few groans, rather than solicit pity for the son. Instead, the father becomes the one to be pitied, not the gay sons—neither the fictional one who moved away and died, nor Williams himself. In the gallery of Williams' leading male characters, Cornelius is an ornery buffoon without precedent. The absent father of *The Glass Menagerie* works neatly as an off-stage antagonist, and it is quite possible that Williams' relationship with his father was too messy in the 1940s for him to have even considered rendering the father as anything but absent. Nearly forty years later, Williams felt comfortable enough in *A House Not Meant to Stand* to draw this father as a comic menace rather than the intensely difficult figure he was in Williams' childhood. By 1982 Williams had come to better terms with his father (who died in 1957) and would have been inclined to portray a man he understood himself to be more like than he had ever realized in his youth. As he expressed in his superb 1960 essay "The Man In The Overstuffed Chair": "I almost feel as if I am sitting in the overstuffed chair where he sat, exiled from those I should love and those that ought to love me."

In an unfinished early draft from 1981, when Williams first began writing the full-length version of the play, he writes of Bella and Cornelius as:

> "The woman—whom I want you to love—and her husband—whom I want you to understand as much as you are able . . ."

Williams could just as easily have been talking about himself instead of the two characters: ". . .as much as you are able . . ." is the key. Williams' recognized his own weaknesses—he had been dramatizing them for decades—but in the dozen years after his release from the psychiatric ward of Barnes Hospital, he gradually began to make peace with some of his demons, and it seems he hoped the public would make peace with them as well.

In another draft fragment, tentatively titled *Our Lady Of Pascagoola*, Williams describes Bella this way:

> "Bella should be presented as a grotesque but heart-breaking Pieta. She all but senselessly broods over the play as an abstraction of human love and compassion—and tragedy . . .
>
> Her entrances and exits, especially while Charlie is with her, should be somewhat formalized. He conducts her on and he conducts her off: a ceremonial effect.
>
> Whenever she appears the play is suspended as all turn

to regard her as if she were indeed an unearthly apparition. Despite the great accretion of flesh, there is a quality of grace and loveliness about her . . ."

Perhaps Hannah from *The Night of the Iguana* most closely corresponds to Bella in her compassion and gentleness. In one important aspect Bella also bears a strong affinity to the first and foremost Tennessee Williams former Southern belle and mother figure, Amanda Wingfield from *The Glass Menagerie*: they are both women obsessed with the past and unable to function in the present without relying on their memories. However, that is where the similarity ends—if anything, Bella could be dubbed the "anti-Amanda," or her counterpoint. Created over thirty-five years later, Bella shares none of Amanda's particular survivor skills, assertiveness or flirtatiousness. Bella treasures her children, and her love for them is unconditional. Amanda treasures her children, and she places all her own failed dreams and hopes on their shoulders, relentlessly pushing them, mostly away from her. Not only is Amanda proud of the beauty she possessed in her youth—as an aging woman she wears her sexuality like a corsage. Not the least concerned with her appearance, Bella overeats and seems to have little or no worry about the excess weight and asthma endangering her health. Amanda's eccentricities are vivid, overbearing, and often charming—she is the kind of character audiences wait on to hear the next droll thing she will say. Bella's eccentricities are low-key; she speaks very little and the measured way she moves through her personal fog is almost unnerving. Bella has the ability to snap out of it and make a sober observation, but then, just as quickly, recede into her more common state of what appears to be mild confusion. Though it is probably something closer to devastating awareness: she can't bear bright lights—the Christmas lights cause her to cry out—she cannot look at her husband or her neighbors most of the time, and she willfully refuses to acknowledge that her oldest son is dead. Although implausible on the surface, Bella's resolve to reclaim her children is, as it turns out, more achievable than Amanda's seemingly more realistic goals. In the face of difficult odds, Amanda fights with the world to give her children the life of which she feels they all have been deprived; she plots, she plans, she is cunning and when her most ambitious scheme ends in failure and the departure of her son, she will rise like a phoenix ready to do it all over again. Bella can also be cunning when she needs to be, but unlike Amanda she turns more and more inward; it is from "spirits" that she draws the moment of happiness she has sought so fervently.

There couldn't be a much more dramatic contrast between the two Williams characters forged in essentially the same fire. In Bella's authentic warmth, there is possibly something of Williams' beloved grandmother, Rose Otte Dakin, who was the most nurturing figure in his childhood. By the time Williams' mother died in 1980, he had long since distanced himself from her emotionally, but as he developed the character of Bella, the death of his mother, Edwina, could not have been far from his mind. Amanda was the ultimate dramatic portrait of Edwina, despite her life-long protests to the contrary. Perhaps Bella is in part an echo of the gentleness that Edwina may have possessed but rarely exhibited.

While the major characters from *The Glass Menagerie* are augmented or inverted in *A House Not Meant to Stand*, the domestic settings in the two plays are strikingly similar. Both consist of a living room, a dining room behind an opaque scrim, a kitchen or part of a kitchen, and a staircase or fire escape. Both spaces have a negative effect on the emotional lives of the families living in them, and each of the scrimmed dining areas is used cinematically to gracefully convey elements of character and plot: the meals and preparations in *The Glass Menagerie*, and Bella's scenes with Charlie, and her spectral children, in *A House Not Meant to Stand*. Both sets function as what Williams referred to as "architectural metaphors"—the former standing in for a cage, and the latter the corrosion of the social order. In both cases Williams brought contemporary political and cultural references directly into the atmosphere of the play. In *The Glass Menagerie*'s opening scene, a sense from the greater world of the 1930s is raised on their St. Louis fire escape by the character of Tom:

> TOM: . . .In Spain there was a revolution. Here there was only shouting and confusion. In Spain there was Guernica. Here there were disturbances of labor, sometimes pretty violent, in otherwise peaceful cities such as Chicago, Cleveland, Saint Louis . . .

In *A House Not Meant to Stand*, Cornelius decries runaway inflation, rising health insurance costs, corrupt government, a weak economy, imperialist aggression, germ warfare and overpopulation. He also turns to the audience and brings the specter of nuclear destruction right into the house with the other living spooks:

> CORNELIUS: . . .—Sinister these times.—East—West—armed to the teeth. —Nukes and neutrons. —Invested so much in every type of munitions, yes, even in germs, cain't afford not to use them, fight it out to the death of every human inhabitant of the earth if not the planet's destruction—opposed by no one . . .

Ultimately, Williams' overarching metaphor of decay—the flesh and blood apparitions, greedy and self-serving, in an imminently collapsing house—reflects, as in a funhouse mirror, our world "house" as he saw it in 1982: full of indifference, cruelty, aggression and potential self-annihilation.

A comedy. The 1982 production of *A House Not Meant to Stand* was fairly well received by the local critics. Glenna Syse of the *Chicago Sun-Times* wrote, "A meticulous honeycomb of a story, with a gossamer heart and a granite spine. This is a playwright who has shed his tears, but you know there's a cackle around the next corner." Richard Christiansen of *The Chicago Tribune,* who reviewed all three incarnations of *House*, was encouraging, though he found the play flawed:

> "From its beginnings, Tennessee Williams' *A House Not Meant to Stand* has never veered from its powerful original impulse. Then, as now, it is a loud, harsh, bitter pain filled shriek at the degenerative process of life . . . [it is] a play that remains, as in its earlier two workshop versions in the Goodman Studio Theater, a tantalizing and frustrating creation."

And, in a comprehensive review of The Miami International Festival of the Arts where the same production of *A House Not Meant to Stand* ran for a week in June of 1982, even *Time* magazine weighed in, calling the play, "The best thing Williams has written since *Small Craft Warnings*." National media attention was needed to extend the life of *A House Not Meant to Stand*, or perhaps move it from Chicago to Broadway, but by then it was too late. For over a decade *Time*, *Newsweek*, *Variety* and *The New York Times* had been reviewing Williams late plays on Broadway, off-off Broadway, and regionally. Their reviews evolved from angry hostile disappointment in the late 1960s to resigned uncomfortable pity in the early 1980s. For an artist who considered himself a bohemian poet/playwright to find himself one of the most successful commercial playwrights of his generation—as Williams did in the 1940s and 1950s—was one thing. But during Williams' lifetime—though quite commonplace today—it was simply unheard of for a commercial playwright of his stature to return to experimentation, or to off-off-Broadway and regional theater. It was more than a demotion: it was inherently a sign of failure. And though Arthur Miller and Edward Albee experienced similar periods of rejection from the critics and the public, each lived long enough to be lauded for his entire body of work.

Neither an attempt to go back to the kinds of plays that had established Williams' reputation, nor one of his overtly experimental plays of the later period (such as *The Remarkable Rooming-House of Mme. Le Monde*), *A House Not Meant to Stand*, stakes its own ground, rather artfully encompassing some of the changes to Williams' style: like a chef with an array of seasonings from which to choose, Williams mixed techniques he had developed over the years. The impressionistic sets for his commercial plays had now become something closer to hyper-realism. In a feature article on the final Goodman production for the *Chicago Tribune*, Williams is quoted:

> "Finally, I think the "German expressionist" treatment was right for my material. I hadn't realized how far I had departed from realism in my writing. I had long since exhausted the so-called "poetic realism." This, after all, isn't twenty years ago."

Emerson and Stacey swing from unlikely extremes of the cartoonish—like characters from *The Gnädges Fräulein* or *Kirche, Küche, Kinder*—to the conventional. Cornelius and Emerson carry on dialogue that verges on the absurd. In spite of the surface familiarity of the domestic setting and its plot elements, *A House Not Meant to Stand* has the structure of a collage: there is no concern in this play about breaking the fourth wall, about raising themes or introducing characters and then dropping them, or about what time it really is, or whether or not there can be ghosts of living people, or where the wraithlike voices are coming from, or whether or not the "men in the white coats" will actually show up to take someone away in the middle of the night, or how the action can come to a standstill in a Mississippi farce. What was truncated or unfinished Beckettian dialogue in *The Bar of a Tokyo Hotel* or *The Two-Character Play* becomes, in *A House Not Meant to Stand,* staccato and yet still complete. And it also bears traces of his former fire, perhaps because he returned to the familiarity of Mississippi cadences such as:

> CHARLIE: How was the funeral, Mom? Did it go off all right?
>
> CORNELIUS: Yeh, perfect.—Grave dug.—Body interred.

Or when Bella is about to run out of the house and into the road:

> EMERSON [*ineffectually attempting restraint*]: Now, now, no, no, Bella. Awful weather outside.
>
> BELLA: INSIDE WORSE!

And there are instances where Williams' language reaches a gothic pitch, such as when senior citizen and recent plastic-surgery patient Jessie Sykes, speaking in her frilly pastel negligee to the audience, rambles from flirtation to death to agony:

> JESSIE: It is a forgivable, understandable sort of deception in a woman with my—sometimes I think almost unnatural attraction to—desire for—sex with young men . . . Spud at the Dock House, he understands the looks I give him and the large tips, he knows what for—expectation! [*She lowers her voice confidingly as she continues speaking to the audience.*] He knows my name, address and phone number!—and so does Mr. Black—that's what I call death . . . Oh, I didn't give it to him, but of course he knows it. Everyone's address is jotted down in his black book, but some for earlier reference than others. Still, I refuse to take cortisone till the pain's past bearing, since it swells up the face which would undo the pain and expense of all those lifts at Ochsner's . . .

A comedy? There are many, many perfectly funny lines in this play, a few sight-gags, a couple of potential pratfalls, some vulgar language, and plenty of sex. But what this play contains in greatest abundance is characters whose lives are filled with grief, pettiness, fear, jealousy, regret and loss. And should you find them funny, well, then, perhaps a nerve has been touched.

Thomas Keith
January 2008

A HOUSE NOT MEANT TO STAND

"Things fall apart; the center cannot hold"
—W.B. YEATS

A House Not Meant to Stand was developed from a one-act play entitled *Some Problems for the Moose Lodge* which was presented on a triple bill with the one-acts *A Perfect Analysis Given by a Parrot* and *The Frosted Glass Coffin* under the collective title *Tennessee Laughs*, and ran at the Goodman Theatre Studio, Chicago, Illinois, from November 8 to the 23, 1980. The evening was directed by Gary Tucker; Artistic Director, Gregory Mosher; Managing Director, Roche Schulfer. The first full-length version of *A House Not Meant to Stand* premiered on April 2, 1981 at the Goodman Theatre Studio, also directed by Gary Tucker.

The final version of *A House Not Meant to Stand*, which is published here, ran from April 16 to May 23, 1982 on the Main Stage at the Goodman Theatre of the Art Institute of Chicago. It was directed by André Ernotte; the set design was by Karen Schulz; the lighting design was by Rachel Budin; costumes were designed by Christa Scholz; sound design was by Michael Schweppe; the stage manager was Joseph Drummond; the assistant stage manager was Marsha Gitkind. The cast in order of appearance, was as follows:

CORNELIUS MCCORKLE	Frank Hamilton
BELLA MCCORKLE	Peg Murray
JESSIE SYKES	Scotty Bloch
CHARLIE MCCORKLE	Scott Jaeck
EMERSON SYKES	Les Podewell
STACEY	Cynthia Baker
TWO MEN FROM FOLEY'S	Brooks Gardner Ed Henzel
OFFICER BRUCE LEE ("PEE WEE") JACKSON	Brooks Gardner
A POLICE OFFICER	Ed Henzel
DR. CRANE	Nathan Davis
HATTIE'S VOICE	Pat Bowie
THREE SPECTRAL CHILDREN:	
YOUNG CHARLIE	Jeremy Sisto
YOUNG JOANIE	Meadow Sisto
YOUNG CHIPS	Jamie Wild

ACT ONE

Midnight, late December of 1982, Pascagoula, Mississippi. The set must establish the genre of the play, which is my kind of Southern Gothic spook sonata. The dilapidation of this house is a metaphor for the state of society. The interior scene should produce a shock of disbelief in the audience. It is as if the panicky disarray and imminent collapse of society were translated into this stage setting which is that of what was once a reasonably, passably, fairly representative middle-class American living room. In brief, it is that which is no more. And we, that participate in it and that are an audience to it, are rightly appalled by this extravagance of 'see-through.'

There is a small entrance hall, a living room with rain-streaked and peeling wallpaper, and a dining room masked by a transparency. The living room contains an overstuffed chair, an armchair, a sofa with end tables, and an old television in a corner. The dining room is visible only at times when significant action takes place in it. Upstage of the dining room a small section of kitchen is visible. There is a staircase that ascends to a landing on which there is a withered palm in a cracked jardinière. The stairs proceed up from the first landing, but are masked above that second flight.

It is a remarkably inclement winter night for the Gulf Coast of Mississippi. Throughout the play, deluges of rain come and go, and there are intermittent rumbles of thunder and flashes of lightning. Sounds of water dripping within the house can occasionally be heard. From time to time, due to a defective power-plant, the lights will flicker: at the end of Act One there will be a total blackout due to the climax of the storm knocking out the power plant for a more extended time.

At the rise of the curtain a large mantel clock ticks rather loudly for about half a minute before there is the sound of persons about to enter the house—the sounds are not vocal but mechanical. The door opens on an old couple who lets themselves into this architec-

tural metaphor from the torrential rain: Cornelius and Bella Mc-Corkle are middle-class, in their late-sixties or early-seventies. The upper frame of Cornelius is slight in comparison to his distended abdomen. Physical descriptions may be flexible—that is, adapted to performance. Bella's way of moving suggests more weight than the actress needs to carry.

Cornelius sets down the luggage with an exhausted grunt and an indignant glance at Bella whose cardiac asthma has incapacitated her for carrying anything much beside her weight. She looks dazed as she will often look during the play. She is holding a large envelope that she wants to conceal from her husband.

CORNELIUS [*to the audience*]: I tell you, entering this house from a cloudburst ain't exactly like coming in outa the rain.

[*Bella wanders into the dining room as Cornelius throws off his coat, dropping it on the floor, and hobbles after her with his cane.*]

CORNELIUS [*to the audience*]: Not tenable this house, not for a man with arthritis. [*To Bella.*] You like it this way? Apparently you do. Since you could easily put on a new roof, afford to easily with a certain cash reserve that's secretly in your possession. Now we're gonna have another talk 'bout that t'night, this time a show-down, Bella. Otherwise—stay alone here. [*To the audience.*] I'll take me a single water-proof room at—somewhere.

[*Bella collides with a chair then leans against the rain-wet table.*]

BELLA: Annh.

[*There are sounds of sexual activity from a bedroom above.*]

STACEY [*from upstairs*]: Nooo, that huuuuuuurts!

CORNELIUS: Wha's that, Bella?

BELLA: Huh?

CORNELIUS: Thought you said somethin'.

BELLA: No, I—said nothing, Cornelius.

CORNELIUS: Somebody in this house?

[*The sounds subside.*]

CORNELIUS: Git your coat off, Bella.

BELLA [*trying to believe her words*]: Good to be home, Cornelius. [*She returns to hang up her coat in the hall.*]

CORNELIUS: —No. —Depressing. [*To the audience.*] So much living gone on in the place none of it come to much more than—[*To Bella.*] thickening of the cartilage in the joints . . . [*To the audience.*] —I hear a leak, several. Never mind. [*To Bella.*] What you took outa the mailbox, Bella? —Advertisement? —Throw it away.

[*Bella shyly, awkwardly stuffs the envelope into her bag.*]

CORNELIUS [*to the audience*]: Encourage—consumerism of unnecessary goods, thrown on the market for no reason but—avarice—insatiable—avarice.

[*Cornelius switches on living room light. A string of colored light bulbs, thrown over the banisters, lights up. Bella utters a sharp cry, covering her face.*]

CORNELIUS: What's that about?

BELLA: Not the Christmas lights!

[*He gives her an exasperated look, then kicks a plug out of double socket: the colored lights go off. He sits in a chair, intermittently groaning and staring out accusingly at the audience. After a pause he addresses Bella.*]

CORNELIUS: Now will you tell me why you hollered like that, Bella?

BELLA [*slowly, with difficulty, as if recalling the details of a vague but terrible dream*]: —Jessie Sykes was here.

CORNELIUS: That bitch comes over here too damn often, drives me upstairs when I can hardly make it . . .

BELLA: You know I can't climb a ladder.

CORNELIUS: Don't get the connection between that fact and—

BELLA: Jessie can.

CORNELIUS: Emerson Sykes is no prize package but I don't see how he can tolerate a bitch that would inherit a small fortune and spend it all on—what? —Rejuvenation? —By cosmetic surgery? Ain't that how she spent it? —Sheee-it, no!

BELLA: Jessie was in the kitchen on the five step ladder getting down that string of colored lights to put on a tree if we got one this Christmas.

CORNELIUS [*half-rising and freezing in position.*]: TYLENOL THREE, TYLENOL THREE!

[*Automatically Bella crosses to him and removes the medication from his jacket pocket.*]

CORNELIUS: Beer to wash it down with.

BELLA: Beer . . .

[*She shuffles ponderously off by the dining room, into the kitchen. Upstairs, unheard by Cornelius but heard by the audience, is the sound of orgasmic rutting. Bella returns with the beer. Cornelius washes the tablet down standing.*]

CORNELIUS: —Jessie Sykes and the ladder—what happened?

BELLA: Took down the lights for—

CORNELIUS: Yeh, yeh, you tole me, Bella.

BELLA [*breathlessly*]: The telephone rung in here. Jessie answered. —It was the call from Memphis. —I thought it was Chips callin' to wish us Merry Christmas maybe even to say he'd be home. —I was comin' out of the kitchen with the lights—Jessie said, "Bella, I think you better talk to this man on the phone." — "Chips? Is it Chips?" —She said she didn't think it was Chips but somebody that knew him and she helped me to the phone. I was dizzy with excitement, could hardly breathe—one of my little attacks . . . I took up the phone. Said "Chips? Is that you, precious?" —Then come on this strange, this hard, cold voice. "Are you Mrs. McCorkle?" —I was scared by the voice—had to set down by the phone. — "Yes, what?" —Man said "I'm afraid I got some bad news for you, Mrs. McCorkle. I'm your son's roommate. —Just come from the hospital. —He's in a deep coma and the doctor admitted it wasn't likely that he'd get through the— [*She cannot continue.*]

CORNELIUS: Night. I know and he didn't.

[*Bella steadies herself against the table.*]

BELLA: Such a hard, cold voice—no emotion in it, no—feeling at all—Chip's roommate? Givin' his mother infalmation like that?

CORNELIUS [*rising, moving slowly toward Bella*]: Yes, that's how they all are, concerned only with self and their dissipations, disgusting practices, aw for Chrissake, thought you knew that by this time. You encouraged it, Bella. Encouraged him to design girls' dresses. He put a yellow wig on and modeled 'em himself. Something—*drag* they call it. Misunderstood correctly—by the neighbors.

BELLA: He could of grown outa that.

CORNELIUS [*rising, moving slowly toward Bella*]: Naw, naw, was in his blood. There was nothin' McCorkle about him, he was pure Dancie and I didn't send him to Memphis, I told him to go stay with your folks, the Dancies, in Pass Christian where sex confusion and outrageous public behavior was not just accepted but cultivated among 'em. Considered essential!

BELLA: —Don't!

CORNELIUS [*touching her shoulder*]: Sorry, it's done, it's past. —This goddamn bone thing's always worse in wet weather. That Memphis specialist says it's osteo-arthritis.

BELLA [*emerging from her trance state*]: —What? [*She moves unsteadily to the sofa and sits down, breathing loudly.*]

CORNELIUS [*sitting in his chair*]: Osteo-arthritis is what he calls it. I asked him how that differed from ordinary arthritis and he couldn't or wouldn't explain. [*Pause.*]

BELLA [*vaguely*]: Maybe age—is the only explanation. [*Pause. The clock ticks loudly.*] Peppy? —Peppy! She's still out in the yard.

CORNELIUS: Let her stay in the yard. I been tellin' you for years that dawg is a yard-dawg. Bella, full of ticks and fleas that get into whatever you sit on so you— [*He scratches his ass.*]

BELLA: Peppy's been with us so long I don't remember and she is family to me.

CORNELIUS: Awright, claim relation with a flea-bitten old mongrel bitch, you do that, but I'll be damned if I'll acknowledge her as an in-law.

[*Jessie Sykes throws open the unlatched front door.*]

JESSIE: Welcome home, neighbors! Knocked at your door, no

response, but I heard your voices, the door was open a crack, so I just considered my self admitted.

CORNELIUS: Is this—Jessie Sykes?

JESSIE: Why, Cornelius McCorkle, that is the nicest thing you've ever said to me. I know what you mean. I am practically unrecognizably transfawned by that cosmetic surgery I went through at Ochsner's, you didn't know who I was!

CORNELIUS [*grudgingly*]: I wasn't *sure* who you was, havin' just took off my glasses.

JESSIE: Bella?

BELLA: Jessie?

[*Jessie embraces her. There is a long pause of embarrassment.*]

JESSIE: I know you must be tired from that sad trip to Memphis.

[*Pause. Bella nods in a dazed fashion and retreats through the arch into the dining room.*]

JESSIE: —I know, I know. —There's nothing to say about it, not tonight, the weather forecast on TV is that it will let up tomorrow, but, Cornelius when are you going to get a new roof on this house?

CORNELIUS: Put that question to Bella.

BELLA: Excuse me, Jessie, can't come in right now

JESSIE: I understand, honey. Oh. Cornelius? Emerson will be dropping over soon. Imagine pretending to me that he was going out possum hunting on a night like this which I know is stag-movie night at the Moose Lodge. You know, he asked Horace Dean to invest in that motel he thinks he's going to put up in Gulfport. And he'll ask you. For heaven's sake, refuse to. Know what he plans to call it? Nite-A-Glory Motel!

[*Cornelius grunts.*]

JESSIE [*to audience*]: You know, Emerson Sykes is fifteen years my senior and is gone into senile dementia of a sexual nature. [*She moves onto the forestage and addresses the audience directly. Light in the living room is dimmed.*] I tell you, it was hilarious as it was disgusting when he drove me over to the construction site. Only the office of it has been erected so far, but a young manager is already employed there. Very attractive, sensible young man. You should have heard the conversation that took place, that young man was bug-eyed with consternation at Emerson's suggestions. It seems they'd already been interviewing applicants for housekeeper. Well. A position like that requires a mature woman, of course, as the young man pointed out—to no avail whatsoever. "No, no, no," Emerson hollered at the fellow. "Get me Gloria Butterfield, you know, that looker, that sexy young looker!" —The poor young man protested that Miss Gloria Butterfield, seventeen years of age, had had no previous employment except as a car-hop at a drive-in! [*She laughs.*]

BELLA [*to audience*]: I don't understand what she is talking about . . .

JESSIE [*to Cornelius and Bella*]: Tell me, do you all expect me to put with that sort of thing? NO, NO, not a bit of it. [*To the audience.*] — "We're entering a period of youth," Emerson hollered.

[*Bella moans.*]

JESSIE: I'm quoting him exactly. "And this motel," he went on, "this prospective chain of motels is designed to keep in close touch with the young, there's no room in it for crones. Now you get Miss

Gloria Butterfield on the phone, if you value your job here, and inform her that the house-keeper position is hers!" —Well, I was so outraged that I snatched up a note-pad on the desk and wrote on this note-pad, "My husband is demented." I slipped that note pad into the young manager's hand. He winked at me and nodded. Then I stalked out of the glorious night motel and drove straight off to Mary Louis Dean's who took me to her law firm. Because I tell you the time has definitely come for legal action. Oh, she's got the same problem, a husband unable to adjust and resign himself to age. And both of us are aware of our legal positions and steps—*steps—must be taken.* [*Away from the audience.*] Cornelius? Have you heard about the sex fiend?

CORNELIUS: The what?

JESSIE: Lock and bolt all the doors. There's a sex fiend at large on the Gulf Coast Highway. It's rumored he's been sighted in a stolen car between here and Cypress Grove. Now, Cornelius, when Emerson drops over, ignore all hints of investment in the Nite-A-Glory Motel. [*She lowers her voice to Cornelius.*] I may phone you later—something is brewing—Bella? Bella? Mary Louise is expecting me at her place now.

BELLA: Oh yes, Mary Louise. Can't see her right now. Maybe later, not tonight, but tomorrow . . .

JESSIE: Bella, you do seem tired. You better retire, get some rest. [*To the audience.*] I talked too much for Bella, she seems so exhausted now. [*To Cornelius.*] Goodbye. [*She goes out the front door. Pause.*]

CORNELIUS: Shit. [*Pause.*] Bella would you get me a . . .

BELLA: Cornelius?

CORNELIUS: Huh?

BELLA [*with unexpected spirit*]: Jessie Sykes told me that you'd told Em that you thought I was gone in the head and had to be removed. —Did you tell that to Em? Is that what you want to do to me? Dispose of my still living remains in a place for gone-in-the-headers? Maybe that's your intention, but you won't find it easy. No, sir. I will put up a fight to wait here for my children which you drove out the door. And this is one intention of mine that will not be defeated by you or anyone else!

[*Cornelius gets up slowly.*]

CORNELIUS: Maybe another beer would make this homecoming less depressin', Bella.

BELLA: I didn't hear that, Cornelius.

CORNELIUS: Too goddamn many afflictions come on at this time of life.

[*He has gone off through the dining room to the kitchen. Voices are heard from upstairs.*]

CHARLIE [*from upstairs*]: Sure, I heard 'em come back.

STACEY [*from upstairs*]: I think we better git dressed. —Cain't tell your clothes from mine all scattered together on the floor. Turn a light on, Charlie.

CHARLIE [*from upstairs*]: No hurry.

STACEY [*from upstairs*]: —What we done, it hurts me. —That's for boys, not—

[*There is an indistinguishable response from Charlie.*]

STACEY [*from upstairs*]: Don't talk about it to no one. Makes a woman feel cheap. —CHARR-LEE!

[*Cornelius returns from the kitchen.*]

BELLA: Cornelius, did you say "Charlie"?

CORNELIUS: Why would I say "Charlie"?

BELLA: Somebody said "Charlie."

CORNELIUS: Me? In the kitchen? Getting' myself a beer?

[*Cornelius falls into his over-stuffed chair with a growl that is reminiscent of the old MGM lion. Bella gasps loudly as she notices a pair of muddy boots by the fireplace.*]

BELLA: Cornelius! Look at what's by the fireplace! Charlie's boots, he's back.

CORNELIUS: Been fired again, I reckon.

BELLA: This late he must be asleep. I'll call him but not loud. [*She goes panting up to the first landing calls.*] Charlie? Charlie?

CORNELIUS: Bella, you been warned to move slow.

CHARLIE [*from upstairs*]: — 'Sthat you, Mom? Are you back?

BELLA: Sweetheart, come down here, baby.

CHARLIE [*from upstairs*]: Comin', Mom—comin'.

CORNELIUS [*to audience*]: Got him that job through my nephew in Yazoo City. Wrote to him, "Jasper, could you possibly make a job for my younger son Charlie in your hardware store? Wouldn't ask this of you except the home situation is desperate with Bella going the Dancie way in her haid and Charlie being—"

STACEY [*from upstairs*]: Charlie, go right down, I got to fix up a little.

CORNELIUS: [*to audience.*] He's got him a woman up there. [*To Bella.*] Brought some hooker here with him!

BELLA: Cornelius, be nice, he didn't expect us this early.

CORNELIUS: This early is late, it's midnight.

[*After a slight pause their younger son, Charlie, about twenty-five, appears on the landing with his undershirt around his neck, struggling into his Levis.*]

BELLA: Baby, baby, seen your boots by the fire, I knew you were home! [*She embraces him, sobbing.*]

CORNELIUS: What's detaining your lady friend upstairs?

CHARLIE [*detaching himself from Bella*]: —Aw, yeh, her, Stacey, my steady in Yazoo City. [*He calls up.*] Come down an' meet my folks, Stacey!

STACEY [*from upstairs*]: Just a few minutes, hon. Have to git into my clo's.

CORNELIUS [*to audience*]: Getting' into her clo's?

CHARLIE: Both of us was so tired we went straight to bed.

CORNELIUS: I bet. —Couldn't wait to.

CHARLIE: How was the funeral, Mom? Did it go off all right?

CORNELIUS: Yeh, perfect. —Grave dug. —Body interred.

BELLA: We'll talk about it tomorrow. I can't discuss it tonight. —You all had supper? Want me to fix you some food? How about an om'lette? Haven't checked the ice-box but think there's eggs.

CHARLIE: That would be wonderful, Mom.

BELLA [*crossing upstage to kitchen door*]: With cheese and tomatoes an' bacon. [*She goes into the kitchen.*]

CORNELIUS: So you lost another job, huh? Discharged by your first cousin!

CHARLIE: That job was misrepresented to me completely.

CORNELIUS: You mean you found it involved some work?

CHARLIE: I don't object to work.

CORNELIUS: As long as you don't have to do it.

STACEY: Psssst!

[*Stacey, Charlie's girl, peeks around the stairs above the top landing, unnoticed except by Charlie who motions her back. She hovers just above the top landing, occasionally peeking around the corner. Her face has a childish appeal. Cornelius lumbers to his easy chair and flops exhaustedly into it, massaging his belly.*]

CHARLIE: —Y'look tired, Pop. How're you feeling?

CORNELIUS: Tired. Sit down, son. While I was in Memphis, burying y'r brother, I wint to a clinic about this chronic digestive trouble of mine. This time I got a genuine diagnosis. It's something called pancreatitis.

CHARLIE: They give you anything for that?

CORNELIUS: Charlie, doctors don't give you nothing but prescriptions and bills and a wagon-load of bullshit, in most cases. However this one impressed me as a possible exception, being a straight-talker. So. I filled the prescription, yep, here's the bottle. —Ever see pills this size?

CHARLIE: Green, huh?

CORNELIUS: What the powder in 'em is made of is a revolting thing. It's the dehydrated and pulverized pancreas of a hawg.

[*Charlie squints at the bottle and spells it out slowly.*]

CHARLIE: C-O-T-A-Z-Y-M-E.

CORNELIUS: Pronounced cotazyme.

CHARLIE: Never heard a that.

CORNELIUS: Three before each meal. Topped off with one of these white tablets here called—what's it say on the bottle?

CHARLIE: D-O-N-N-A-T-A-L.

CORNELIUS: That's it. Three big greens and one of the little whites for abdominal distress. Offered me some relief but the expense is awful. When a man's got to live off pills in the quantity at the price, extortionary, with only temporary relief at best, why, I say it's time to quit hangin' on, it's time for a man to let go.

CHARLIE: If you feel that way about it, why that's your decision, huh, Pop?

CORNELIUS: Damn right it is. And no concern of nobody but mine.

CHARLIE: —Under these circumstances, Pop, I hope it ain't true that you allowed your insurance to run out.

CORNELIUS: With inflation completely out of control, I refuse to pay the new rates. People in this country have got to learn to refuse to pay more and more for ev'ry commodity or service which they purchase, including insurance rates.

CHARLIE: You've got Mom to think of.

CORNELIUS: You think a woman that pants louder'n an ole yard dog is going to outlive me? Doctor tole me privately that if she'd quit stuffin' and bring down her weight, she could go on a year longer, but she won't, no way, no way.

CHARLIE: You got no concern for her, then?

CORNELIUS: There's cases in which continued existence is not desirable, Charlie. I mean when the mind is gone.

[*Bella appears behind the dining room scrim, setting silverware on the table.*]

CORNELIUS: A woman in her condition is not responsible for peculiar behavior and so you can't blame her for it. Now, Charlie, excuse me for discussin' your mother's folks which is half yours, too, but a good deal of this is hereditary with Bella. [*He moves to join Charlie on the sofa.*] I mean, you know the Dancies. Ev'ryone on the Gulf Coast knows about the Dancies. Lunacy runs rampant among them, son. Was you old enough to remember that time your mother's sister walked naked out of the house at high noon with just a hat on and the hat was a man's? Sex confusion existed among them, Charlie, never among the McCorkles. Your just buried brother did not take after me, pathetic creature, typical of the Dancies.

CHARLIE: Not so loud, Pop, Mom's in the dinin' room, list'nin.

CORNELIUS: Charlie, I reckon you heard of the Dancie money?

[*Bella goes back into the kitchen.*]

CHARLIE: Yeh. —I heard that it was Confederate money—old Confederate bills.

CORNELIUS: Well, it ain't Confederate money and I know how it was made. By bootleg liquor durin' prohibition, that's how and when and it was made by Old Grannie Dancie in the pine woods back of the house. Old Grannie Dancie was the only one in the bunch had any get up an' go.

CHARLIE: So she got up and went into bootleg liquor, huh, Pop?

CORNELIUS: Yep. Got to admire the ole bag, supported the whole tribe of 'em for a generation on money from bootleggin'. Never banked what was left of that money. Say she kept it in the house but bein' conscious when she died of the Dancie sickness at eighty something—

CHARLIE: Dancie sickness is what?

CORNELIUS: Over indulgence either in food like Bella or liquor like Grannie Dancie. Over indulgence is the Dancie sickness. Your older sister, Joanie, indulged in too much fornication, such a scandal had to throw her out. Now Charlie? There is a rumor not unlikely at all that your Mom's got the Dancie money.

CHARLIE: Hell, she woulda mentioned it. How much is it?

CORNELIUS: They say it's a big wad of thousand dollar bills, at least a coupla hundred thousand dollar bills and it's just possible that your Mom's got it. More'n possible, Charlie.

CHARLIE: —Where?

CORNELIUS: I have tried to find out for fifteen years. Jesus! When I mention it to her she just looks sly. Oh, Bella knows how to be sly. That's part of the Dancie sickness—crazy but cunning and sly. Now, Charlie. She couldn't of banked it locally without me knowing, so she's probably got it hid somewhere and it would be a terrible thing if she wint to her grave anytime now without passing it on.

CHARLIE: —To *who*? —To *you*?

CORNELIUS: Look. I supported her all these years, supported her stuffing, and the scandal of Chips and the scandal of Joanie, oh, I've earned the right to that Dancie money by patience past all belief, all reasonable endurance. Of cou'se some of it would natcherly go to you, Charlie.

CHARLIE: —How much of it, Pop?

CORNELIUS: After I git in office—

CHARLIE: Aw, you want to throw it away on political campaigns that git you nowhere, Pop? Never did, never will!

CORNELIUS: —Charlie, a man in Congress has many opportunities to make money outside of his salary. —My campaigns had no financial backing. This time, *with* the Dancie money . . .

CHARLIE: But if the Dancie money exists and it's in Mom's hands, you want it, don't you? Ain't that what you're after, Pop?

CORNELIUS: Goddamn it, sure I want what's rightfully mine. Now, Charlie. —You want a political job? —Something simple that you could handle without much effort? —You got it. —But first, Charlie, you got to persuade your Mom to tell you what she's done with the Dancie money. Otherwise, by God, I'll have to tear this house down board from rotten board to find where she hid it when she's fallen victim to indulgence like the others. You know the Dancies over there in Pass Christian have torn that two and a ha'f story frame house apart tryin' to find that wad of thousand dollar bills? The house is a regular shambles inside, no partitions at all, and they're still at it. Why, it's fifteen years since Grannie Dancie's widower past on. They thought he had it cause he never removed his right hand from his pants pocket. He died in his pants, same pair, never changed. However. I happen to know that Bella was in the Dancie house when he died, alone in the bedroom with him, and he favored Bella. Shay-it! Sly? But you're the only son, now. She knows she's goin'. C'mon, get with it, Charlie. Be nice to your Mom and she will give it to you or tell you where it is.

CHARLIE: For you to blow on runnin' for Congress with no pancreas, Pop, an' hobbling on a stick? Ha, no way, forget it.

CORNELIUS: No patriotism in you? This Congressional district needs a McCorkle. —To disclose the lies that betrayed the Democracy into rich—Imperialism of about ten or a dozen of big families and conglomerates profiting from— [*Lurches up from chair and hobbles to the audience.*] WAR! —IMPERIALIST AGGRESSION

AND YOU KNOW IT, THAT'S RIGHT, ALL OF YOU KNOW IT! —SUCKERS . . . [*He returns to his chair, grumbling.*]

CHARLIE: Pop? —You're a card, the funny card in the deck. I think you better shut up about runnin' for awfice in Pascagoula, I think you better shut up about the Dancie money, too, 'cause even if Mom's got it and told me where it was—think I'd let you know?

[*Bella goes back into the dining room to set napkins, etc. at the table.*]

CORNELIUS [*placing an arm over Charlie's shoulder*]: —Son?

CHARLIE: 's too late to butter me up that "Son" crap. Mom had three children—you don't acknowledge a one. —Chips was my brother, Joanie's my sister—you're no relation to me.

CORNELIUS: —Not a McCorkle?

CHARLIE: Rather be a Dancie.

CORNELIUS: Awright, be a Dancie. But git the Dancie money out of your Mom before she kicks the—

CHARLIE: Not so loud—Mom's in the dining room.

CORNELIUS: List'nin' to her blood-pressure, son. She complains it roars in her ears like a stawn sometimes.

CHARLIE: She's leanin' against the table in the dinin' room.

CORNELIUS: Never mind, she heard nothin'. Speak to her. You'll see.

CHARLIE: Mom? Are you all right in there, Mom?

BELLA [*leaning on the dining room table*]: I grated come Onions for the om'lette. I'll bring it out as soon as—om'lette's got to be watched—excuse me, won't take long. [*She starts back toward kitchen but staggers dizzily against wall.*]

CORNELIUS: Help her, seems to be— [*He sits.*]

[*Charlie enters the dim dining room area.*]

CHARLIE: Mom?

BELLA: —Chips?

CHARLIE: No, no, Mom, I'm Charlie.

BELLA: Sorry—yes, you're Charlie

CHARLIE: Go in front, set with Pop, he's not well. I'll take care of the om'lette.

BELLA: I cook for my men folks and will till I die, son.

CHARLIE: I know Mom, but tonight, I think you oughta go in front with Pop. He seems tired and depressed about something. So just go make yourself comfortable on the sofa and sympathize with Pop about—he's got new medical problems. Are you all right?

[*Slowly, ceremonially, Charlie conducts Bella into the living room. He gently releases his hold on her before the sofa. She falls onto it as if struck dead.*]

CORNELIUS: Bella? Bella?

[*Scene freezes a moment or two.*]

CORNELIUS: Can you hear me, Bella?

BELLA: I hear a terrible stawm. Chips insisted I let him prepare the om'lette, sweet.

CORNELIUS [*to audience*]: Chips insisted! You hear that?

BELLA: Always such a sweet boy. [*She picks up a large, leather framed, hand-tinted photo of Chips, hair blond in ringlets, long neck, wide baby-blue eyes.*] Remember when he was voted the handsomest boy at Pascagoula High?

CORNELIUS: I remember when he was voted the prettiest girl at Pascagoula High. That I remember clearly.

CHARLIE: Pop, you know the, the—editor of the class annual just, he—got it mixed up, a—accidental mix-up.

BELLA: What's that? I didn't unnerstand that, Chips.

CORNELIUS [*slowly and loudly*]: Bella, do you realize you're talkin' to Charlie, not Chips, whose funeral we attended a day ago in Memphis?

[*There is a slight pause.*]

BELLA: Charlie? Not Chips? —Tragedy, long trip. No sleep.

CHARLIE [*sitting next to her*]: Confused you a little, Mom.

BELLA: I only know I got three precious children to thank God faw. Oh, the om'lette could scawch! Not sure if . . . [*She gets up from the sofa.*]

CORNELIUS: Charlie, you reckon you could get her back to the kitchen where she seems to be headed? —Did you hear me, Charlie?

[*Bella goes back into the kitchen.*]

CHARLIE: You know, I think we need somebody to help her out, a—a able—bodied young woman to—

CORNELIUS: What people need and what people can afford are two diff'rent things.

CHARLIE: Well, if I got married, for instance—

CORNELIUS: Unemployed? —First get a job you can hold, then think about matrimony.

CHARLIE: Pop, I know your retirement pay was adequate when you received it, but hasn't kept up with this run-away inflation.

CORNELIUS: Hell, what could keep pace with it except a hawss that won the Kentucky Derby by ten lengths?

CHARLIE: Some people think we're haided into depression. 'Sthat your opinion?

CORNELIUS: Opinion, no, conviction, yais. [*To the audience.*] It's not the President's fault but the fault of the system which don't adjust to the population increase, here and world over, too many stomachs to feed. Why, I read somewhere that by the year 2030, which you might survive to enjoy, world population will have doubled. I'm glad I'll be departed. Oh, they tole me when I run for Mayor of Pascagoula on the Independent ticket, I hadn't the chance of a fart in a wind-stawm with a radical opinion such as that, but I don't compromise with principles and convictions and so got only ten votes out of two hundred at the Moose Lodge. [*To Charlie.*] Why, even your Mom said she couldn't git to the polls though offered transportation and still in reasonable health.

CHARLIE [*suppressing a grin*]: Ten votes only for Mayor of Pascagoula. Sorry about that, Pop.

CORNELIUS: I don't regret it. Who needs political office in times like this? Only crooks that line their pockets with bribes.

CHARLIE: Might have been profitable to you. However this house is a piece of Gulf Coast property, Pop.

CORNELIUS: This house is held up, why it's literally supported by termites!

CHARLIE: House, maybe, but not the grounds. What would it be worth if we was obliged to sell it when you, if you ever—after you've—

CORNELIUS: Departed? —Why are you so int'rested in my value as a cadaver?

CHARLIE: You misunderstand me completely. It just seem to me—

[*There is knock at the door.*]

CORNELIUS: *Charlie!*

[*Another knock at door—pause.*]

CORNELIUS: See who's at the door, just across the room there.

CHARLIE [*bristling*]: You tellin' me where the door is?

CORNELIUS: Thought you might not've noticed its location.

[*The door is still slightly ajar. A sharp, sly-featured old man about the age of Cornelius stalks in. He is in rubber boots and hunting clothes.*]

EMERSON: Never mind gettin' up. The door wasn't shut. —Well, —How is the old hound-dawg?

CORNELIUS [*stopping short with displeasure*]: —Em, we been neighbors and Lodge brothers for a long time.

EMERSON: Yep, we sure have, um-hmmm.

CORNELIUS: Em, I don't mind you addressin' me as the ole hound-dawg in private, however lately you have taken to callin' me that in public.

EMERSON: Heh-heh. So?

CORNELIUS: So, I *do* object to being called an ole hound-dawg in public.

EMERSON [*grinning*]: —What's your objection to it? —Strikes you as too familiar?

CORNELIUS: Em, you know that I am a man in politics now.

EMERSON: Heh heh, no.

CORNELIUS: Then what did you think I was in?

[*The phone rings. Cornelius hobbles to the phone.*]

EMERSON: Retirement, Corney.

CORNELIUS [*into the phone*]: McCorkle residence. —Yes, he is, Mrs. Sykes, he just arrived here. —I'll tell him. [*He hangs up.*]

EMERSON: Jessie! —Tell me what?

CORNELIUS: You left your key so you'll have to stay till she's back from Mary Louise's.

EMERSON: Pair of bitches, constantly together.

CORNELIUS: So! —You consider me in retirement! Well. I am in retirement. [*Addressing the audience.*] From the vice-presidency of the Pascagoula Ice Plant despite being offered the presidency of it by T. C. Wallow after his second stroke immobilized him so completely. Even took to going there on Sundays and—yep, Saturdays and Sundays had his boy deliver him at the ice plant, opened up the deserted building, staggered back to his chair and stared out the window till it was totally black. Sometimes the boy fawgot to pick him up and he would consequently remain there all night, unable to git to the tawlit or not bothering to. Oh, there's a lot of terrible details about the last years of T. C. Wallow which I don't care to go into. He's well out of it now. Retired from existence too late to avoid what I call the disposition of the living remains.

[*Thunder and rain are heard.*]

CORNELIUS: —However— [*He turns to Emerson.*] You just indicated to my astonishment, Em, that you had no idea that I was in politics now. Very surprising and alarming oversight on your part since I've run several times for office and assumed you'd voted for me.

[*Emerson gives Charlie a puzzled look.*]

CHARLIE: Mr. Sykes, Pop's just come back from a funeral in Memphis.

EMERSON: Sure, sure, I understand your Pop, Charlie. How you doin', boy?

CHARLIE: Fine, thank you, Mr. Sykes, set down.

EMERSON: I seen your lights on, I just dropped over to see if I could be of any assistance.

CHARLIE: Been out huntin' in this wet weather?

EMERSON: Heh heh, naw, just a pretext to fool the old lady. They had stag movies at the Lodge tonight. [*He winks.*] Corney, I'm mighty put out with Jessie right now. She come into some money from her oldest brother who finally died. That money could of been useful in financin' the motel over at Gulfport. Could of been but wasn't. Goddamn if she didn't blow the whole wad on—Jesus! —a series of operations she thinks has returned her youth to her—I ain't spoke much to her since. —Could you spare me some a that beer?

CORNELIUS: Sure, sure, but why dontcha put your gun down—unless y'come over with homicidal intentions, ha ha. Charlie, set his gun down. *Hey, Charlie. Can you hear me?*

[*Charlie takes Em's gun and sets it against the wall beside the what-not shelves.*]

CORNELIUS: Charlie's got his mind upstairs with some female he snuck home with him from Yazoo City.

EMERSON: Did he now? Nothing wrong with that. That's understandable, Corney.

BELLA [*coming out of the kitchen*]: Lucky I discovered more eggs in the ice-box since I burnt the first batch. [*Bella crosses through the dining room.*] Why, that's Emerson Sykes in here!

EMERSON: Yes, I come to express my sympathy, Bella.

BELLA: Scuse me, got eggs frying. I'll come in later. [*She returns to the kitchen.*]

CORNELIUS: Probably devoured that first om'lette herself. You hungry, Em?

EMERSON: Naw, naw, had a big barbecue supper, I could use a beer though.

CORNELIUS: Charlie, go get a coupla cold beers from the frig.

[*Charlie glances up at the stair landing as Stacey's head appears, then crosses in a deliberate manner and goes into the kitchen.*]

CORNELIUS: Set down, Em.

EMERSON: My clo's are damp.

CORNELIUS: Probably dryer than the furniture. Wow, imagine! —Bella's fryin' up more food.

[*The repetitive and somewhat confused long-winded speeches of Cornelius can be used as a comic dynamic: they should be delivered with an unctuous drawl. Although a certain sympathy exists between Corney and Em through long association in a small town, They have really stopped listening to each other.*]

CORNELIUS: Y'know I used t' let 'er walk to the Kwik-Chek.

EMERSON: Didja?

[*Emerson glances up at Stacey as she pops her head around the turn of the stairs. She does this periodically to see if the stage is set for her appearance. Bella has come out of the kitchen and is always dimly visible in the dining room area.*]

CORNELIUS: Yep. Just two blocks and a half from the house. They say a little exercise is beneficial to overweight people with cardiac asthma like Bella, you know, long as it ain't a climb but on level ground.

EMERSON: So Charlie come home with a young lady. Must be serious. Is she a looker?

CORNELIUS: Gettin' into her clo's. [*There is a considerable, gloomily ruminative pause.*] —What was I talking about?

EMERSON: You said she's getting into her clo's.

CORNELIUS: Naw, naw, Em, you just don't *listen*! I was talkin' about the—whadaya call it? Market, market, chain market? Funny how familiar names slip your mind sometimes like this—aw, KWIK-CHEK!

[*Bella enters from the dim dining room.*]

BELLA: All right, Cornelius. Where'd I put my coat, just let me get into my coat.

CORNELIUS: Bella, you going out somewhere?

BELLA: I thought you said the Kwik-Chek. Is it time?

[*Cornelius gives Emerson an incredulous look. Then leads Bella to a position facing the blank-faced clock.*]

CORNELIUS: Can you see the clock, Bella—BELLA, CAN YOU SEE THE CLOCK?

BELLA: —*Twelve*! —You should've called me, Cornelius.

CORNELIUS: For what?

BELLA [*panicky*]: *Kwik-Chek?!*

[*Charlie stands center stage, opening and closing his fists.*]

CORNELIUS: Kwik-Chek? After midnight?

CHARLIE: Pop, you gotta take it easy on Mom. [*He places an arm about Bella.*] Mom, why don't you get you some sleep? Why don't you stretch out downstairs tonight and Pop an' Mr. Sykes can talk in the kitchen where the beer is? Huh?

BELLA: One thing I won't stop doing is shopping for the house. [*To the audience.*] When I can't go out shopping, why, then I better give up, I—

EMERSON: This is not a usual sort of night. You got to consider that, Corney.

CHARLIE: Mom, let's go back in the kitchen. You can stretch out on the cot that old Hattie used. I'll bring it outa the woodshed.

BELLA: Woodshed? [*She returns to the kitchen with Charlie following.*]

[*Cornelius moans.*]

EMERSON: Corney, you're tired out from the trip to Memphis, I know, but even before then, for some time now, I notice you've got into a habit of saying a thing and then repeating it not just once but two or three times more.

CORNELIUS [*cutting in*]: You want to know why I repeat myself a couple of times when I am talking to you, Em? It's because you don't hear me the first time. Your mind is distracted by some problem with this motel which Mosley, the vice-president of the bank, told me you're likely to—hate to tell you this but this is what he told me! —you took out a loan at that ridiculous twenty percent interest rate and Mosley says that he don't see how you can meet the payments on it.

[*This gets through to Emerson, who draws himself up.*]

EMERSON [*cutting in*]: Corney, do you realize that it's no goddamn business of yours to discuss my financial affairs with—

CORNELIUS: Didn't discuss 'em! Mosley brought up the subject to me at the last Progress Club meeting and asked me if I could warn you.

EMERSON: Awright, you have delivered this warning. Now let me assure you and that asshole Mosley that never in my life as a highly successful realtor, owner of Sykes and Sykes Refinery and now as owner-to-be of the outstanding motel *chain* on the Coast, never once have I failed to pay off every goddamn cent that I've—

CORNELIUS: I will tell Mosley—

EMERSON: Tell Mosley nothing! I'll call Jack Saterlee in the mawnin and assure him that if there is any anxiety over my ability to pay off that loan, I will pay it off at once, six months before due!

CORNELIUS: Em, I sincerely hope and pray that Black Jack Saterlee don't take you up on that offer if you're such a fool as to make it. In order to secure that loan you had to submit a complete list of your assets, such as they were or would be in your opinion. He knows 'em, the existing ones, down to your three-year-old, naw, naw, five-year-old Caddy, and wasn't it bought second hand? "Show me a man in a second hand Caddy, a 1977 Caddy in 1982, parking in the Gulf Coast Bank and Trust lot, and I'll show you a man that's about to perpetrate a con compared to which the Pidgin

Drop and the Jamaica Switch is innocent child's play." Em, I'm quoting his exact words because I think you should know them.

CHARLIE [*coming from the kitchen to the dining room arch*]: Not so loud, Pop. Mom is feeling anxious and confused.

EMERSON: Tell your Mom, son, she's got every reason to be anxious and confused Her husband is—a little touched.

[*There is noise from the kitchen.*]

CORNELIUS: Is what?

CHARLIE: Just not so loud, huh, Pop, she's stumbling around in circles in the kitchen, knocking things over.

STACEY [*from upstairs*]: Charlie—will you please bring me up my suitcase?

[*Stacey sticks her head around the stairs. Emerson sees her and winks.*]

CORNELIUS: Go back there and set her down. I am trying to talk some sense into Emerson Sykes. Now—DO I HAVE YOUR ATTENTION? WHY ARE YOU STARING UP THOSE STAIRS, YOU WANTA GO TO THE TAWLIT OR TAKE A GANDER AT CHARLIE'S GIRLFRIEND, THE OVERNIGHT GUEST FROM YAZOO CITY?

CHARLIE: FOR CHRISSAKE, DAD, SHUDDUP!

CORNELIUS: Git your ass out of here and bring in the rest of the beer.

[*Charlie goes into the kitchen.*]

CORNELIUS: Em? —EM!

EMERSON: Now what?

CORNELIUS: Mosley has also been interested in your preceding enterprises and is trying to check them out. Right now it's his impression, and frankly everyone else's, that you went broke at both, at least declared bankruptcy.

EMERSON: BROKE YOUR ASS! ME? WINT BROKE? GOD-DAMN IF MOSLEY DARES TO MAKE AN ASSERTION LIKE THAT IN MY PRESENCE I'LL HAUL HIM TO COURT FOR—

[*Charlie appears in the dining room archway.*]

CORNELIUS [*staggering up and gripping Emerson's shoulders*]: Let's talk this over quietly like old neighbors and Lodge Brothers, not, not shout about court which is what you better try to keep out of. However—

[*Charlie starts toward stairs with remaining six-pack.*]

CORNELIUS: Charlie, where are you haided with them beers? Upstairs to Miss Yazoo City? Bring those beers right here. One for Mr. Sykes, one for me, and set the rest down.

[*Charlie hands them the beers. Cornelius and Emerson sit. Charlie goes back into the kitchen.*]

EMERSON: Corney, there's a difference between going broke and declaring bankruptcy. There happened to be tax-advantages in declaring these firms bankrupt when I had awready decided to convert all capital assets into this chain of motels I'm planning. Corney, you've never been involved in the manipulation of large sums of money. Money is a thing that any successful business man knows has to be manipulated skillfully.

CORNELIUS: If by skillfully you mean illegally in any way, don't enlighten me on it. I desire no knowledge of any manipulations in sums of money large or small or none whatsoever as the case may be.

EMERSON [*standing*]: MONEY.

CORNELIUS: What about money? Aside from losing all value?

EMERSON: MONEY. M-O-N-E-

CORNELIUS [*standing*] : Hell, I know how to *spell* it!

EMERSON: MONEY!

CORNELIUS: Awright, money, continue from there.

[*Both men resume their seats.*]

EMERSON: I don't want to talk about my financial operations with you, Corney, or with anyone not experienced with large-scale operations such as—Sykes and Sykes Realtors, Sykes and Sykes Refinery and—

CORNELIUS: Did you say refinery?

[*There is a pregnant pause. Emerson is disconcerted*]

EMERSON: Refinery, yais, refinery, Sykes and Sykes Refinery.

CORNELIUS: Sykes and Sykes. Don't you realize, Em, that nobody on the Gulf Coast knows who this other Sykes is and some suspected and expressed the suspicion that he does not exist and did never?

[*Emerson fixes him with a silent, astonished stare as the living room area dims slightly.*]

BELLA [*emerging from kitchen with Charlie*]: —So dark in here, son. Switch the lights on, please.

CHARLIE [*touching switch*]: They don't come on. —Maybe it's the fuse.

BELLA: I didn't catch that.

CHARLIE: Check it later. Right now I'll light the candles.

[*Bella refers to a badly tarnished candelabra on the dining room table*]

BELLA: Yes, please do that, Chips.

CORNELIUS [*from his chair*]: Hear that in there, Em? Imagine living continually with a woman out of her mind! Alone in a house with a woman out of her mind! Dangerous! Never know when a lunatic will turn violent . . .

[*Charlie strides quickly to dining room arch as light brightens on living room.*]

CHARLIE: If Mom is in a bad mental condition, after the funeral—

CORNELIUS: Long, long before.

BELLA [*crossing into living room, eating something in a bowl.*] What's—

[*Bella sways. Charlie places an arm about her.*]

CHARLIE: Set down in the dining room, Mom. I want to say something privately to Pop.

CORNELIUS: Do you? Well, say it!

[*Bella has gone back into the dining room area. Picks up the candelabra and staggers about the table, gazing around with an air of disbelief and loss past enduring.*]

CHARLIE: —I—I

STACEY [*poking her head around the upper stairs*]: Charlie! Suitcase! —Cain't find it.

CORNELIUS: You're being paged by your Yazoo City import. There's an embargo against her kind here in my house.

CHARLIE: You! —Later, I'll talk to you later . . . [*He returns to Bella, in the weirdly candle-lit dining room.*]

EMERSON: Your boy was almost cryin', Corney, there was tears in his eyes.

CORNELIUS: I don't respect tears in a man, and over-attachment to Mom, Mom, Mom. Very strange. He and Chips had a lot in common except for the sex thing. Oh, both insatiable for it, but him one way, Chips the other . . .

[*Bella picks up the candelabra.*]

CORNELIUS: 'Scuse me.

EMERSON: Going?

CORNELIUS: Just for a look at the weather. [*He hobbles onto the forestage, clutching his abdomen and bends over. Lights go down in living room, and up in dining room.*]

CHARLIE: You lookin' for something, Mom?

[*Holding the tarnished candelabra, Bella continues to stare about in a bewildered way.*]

CHARLIE: What are you lookin' for, Mom?

BELLA: —Life, all the life that we had here!

CHARLIE: —But nothing in particular?

BELLA: The life. —In particular? Yes, something. —See? —Just two chairs at the table since you children been gone. Cornelius insisted the other chairs go out, said the empty chairs at the table—depressed—unnecessary—removed them. Well, now, I want them all back here. I want five chairs at this table. They are out in the woodshed—I want them back in here! This fam'ly is returned! All! —Chips? Let Charlie do it. You are tired tonight, son, after—

CHARLIE [*abruptly*]: Mom? I'm Charlie. Not tired—I'm perfectly able to bring in the chairs from the woodshed. [*He goes into the kitchen.*]

BELLA: Not, not—t'night, rest up from your—long trip.

CORNELIUS [*on the forestage*]: Terrible—abdominal—distress. Maybe another Donna— [*He fumbles in his pocket, finds the Donnatel tablets, spills them on floor.*] —Hell's—fire! [*He descends slowly, groaning, to his knees.*] Collect others—later . . . [*He takes a tablet and returns to the living room.*]

EMERSON: Something wrong, Corney?

CORNELIUS: Something—I got to get accustomed to, Em.

[*Bella, holding the black and silver speckled candelabra, wanders to the arched dining room entrance.*]

CORNELIUS: —You looking for something, Bella?

BELLA: Yes—No . . . Em . . . [*She turns back into the dining room. A faint phrase of music is heard as she stands still a moment, a phrase from a childhood game entering the slow drift of her mind.*] Heavy, heavy—hangs over the head—or the heart? —and what shall the owner do—to redeem it . . . !

[*Cornelius opens a beer.*]

EMERSON: Huh?

CORNELIUS: Common experience begins to seem—

EMERSON: Strange . . .

CORNELIUS: —My father Chipton McCorkle put me through college—Loyola? —Did. I wonder if education is practiced much anymore.

[*Emerson rises.*]

CORNELIUS: —Naw, don't go . . .

[*Emerson resumes his seat.*]

CORNELIUS: Drink your beer, Em. Did Charlie ever bring a opener in?

EMERSON: Opener? For screw-top bottles?

[*Light goes down in the living room, up in the dining room.*]

BELLA [*recalling other phrases of games*]: —Dog takes the cat, cat takes the rat, rat take the cheese—and the? —cheese stands alone . . .

[*There are sounds from kitchen. Charlie enters lugging a couple of dining room chairs.*]

BELLA: Oh, you found—!

CHARLIE: Yes, Mom.

BELLA: Don't, don't strain, get a—rupture—all three chairs?

CHARLIE: Two, Mom, and the cot for Hattie.

BELLA: Is she—? —Hattie . . .

CHARLIE: Hope there's some dry sheets in the house so you can sleep on it, Mom.

BELLA: Remember how we joked about Hattie coming from Hattiesburg, Charlie?

CHARLIE: Yeh. Named for it or it was named for her.

BELLA: Just two chairs, not three?

CHARLIE: Other's out there, I'll git it.

BELLA [*her mind drifting*]: Chips, it broke my heart when Cornelius drove you an' little Joanie out of the house. Try to forgive but can't. You're wet, baby, change into dry things right away, always caught cold so easy.

CHARLIE: Yep, did, easy, I'll bring in the other chair. [*Charlie goes into the kitchen.*]

BELLA: —Good . . . Something else that's missing, something else—been removed— [*There is a pause. Her breath is audible, she is clutching the edge of the table.*] —Most precious thing we ever had in this house. Can see it with my eyes shut, every detail nearly, getting clearer and clearer, so clear!

CHARLIE [*entering*]: Here's the other chair, Mom.

BELLA: Chips, the picture of Gramps and Grannie's Gold Anniversary Picnic, summer of 1930!

CORNELIUS [*from the living room*]: Another commotion, endless . . .

BELLA [*at the arch, to Cornelius*]: You! Did you put it away because Chips loved it so much, because it was so much admired by all the children you concealed it, did you?

[*Emerson coughs self-consciously. Cornelius addresses Charlie.*]

CORNELIUS: Get her settled somewhere. Don't know what she's talkin' about and doubt that she does either. It's long overdue—commitment.

CHARLIE [*shepherding Bella back into the dining room again*]: I remember it, Mom, just noticed it in the woodshed.

BELLA: Him in there, he committed it to the woodshed. Did you hear him say commitment? Long overdue?

CHARLIE [*as he exits to the kitchen*]: Set tight, Mom, I'll git it.

STACEY [*forlornly, from upstairs*]: Cain't find my suitcase.

EMERSON [*in the living room*]: No lights in that room?

CORNELIUS: Burnt out . . .

EMERSON: Burnt?

CORNELIUS: Out.

EMERSON: Oh.

CORNELIUS: Em, I'll need some witnesses to her condition to git her removed and I count on you to stand by me.

CHARLIE [*enters the dining room from the kitchen*]: Here it is, Mom.

BELLA: The nail is still in the wall, hang it back up, Chips, honey.

CORNELIUS [*in the living room*]: Make a note of it. Refers to Charlie as Chips.

EMERSON: I couldn't stand by you in putting that woman away—no more'n you'd stand by putting me away or me stand by putting you away. There is too much putting away of old and worn-out people. Death will do it for all. So why take premature action?

[*Meanwhile, in the dining room—*]

BELLA: Need my glasses, in purse . . .

[*Charlie enters the living room.*]

CORNELIUS: Well?

CHARLIE: Mom's purse. Aw. Here. [*He returns to the dining room, and removes the glasses from her purse. Bella takes them and drops them from her trembling hands.*]

BELLA: Oh, God, broken?

CHARLIE: No, Mom. [*He puts them on her.*]

BELLA: Thanks, baby. Now just bring me the candles. A little bit closer. [*The large tinted photo is lighted.*] Ahhhhhh . . . . [*She bursts into tears.*]

CHARLIE: Set down, Mom.

BELLA: Heart-breaking! Picture's so dim it's hardly visible, Chips . . .

CHARLIE: Aw. I see the problem. [*He removes a tissue from her purse, wipes lenses of glasses.*]

CORNELIUS [*in living room*]: Em, are you observing?

EMERSON: No. I don't approve of it.

CORNELIUS: Then fuck off.

EMERSON: Fuck off, yourself.

CORNELIUS: Sorry. Excuse. 'nother beer?

STACEY [*from upstairs*]: Charlie, Charlie, you down there?

EMERSON: When is she going to grace us with her appearance?

CORNELIUS: Her up there? A prostitute in my house?

CHARLIE [*in the dining room*]: —Can you make it out now?

BELLA: Yes, this is it, not in perfeck condition—whole Dancie family, summer of 1930, the Gold Anniversary picture. See? See? —My eyes keep clouding over with—time . . . 1930 to what? Years? Now? [*She removes her glasses.*]

CHARLIE: Much later, Mom—fifty, fifty-two years . . .

BELLA: Impossible to imagine such passage of time . . . [*Voice gathering a rhapsodic power.*] All, all, all gathered together about—old Gramp's skatterbolt we called it.

CORNELIUS [*from the living room*]: Delirious shouting!

BELLA [*swaying like a religieuse*]: See the number, the many, present for the occasion, the Gold Anniversary of it, not all of 'em Dancies, but girlfriends and boyfriends attended! —All embracing, so happy, that long ago— [*Gasps.*] Time . . . [*Gasps.*] Committed? [*Gasps.*] No. Not a one of them . . . Reported falsely by gossip. There, there is Grannie Dancie, look at her smiling!

CORNELIUS: Grinning like a possum eating shit.

BELLA [*turning her back to him*]: What was that remark about Grannie Dancie he made?

CHARLIE: Nothing I'd repeat to you, it was too dirty.

BELLA: Don't! —That man is full of hate as the Dancies was full of love!

CORNELIUS [*getting up*]: And moonshine money, that's what the Dancie's were full of!

EMERSON: Easy, easy with Bella. Wonderful woman, much loved here.

[*Cornelius comes to the archway.*]

BELLA: Chips, call me a cab. Jessie Sykes told me he wants me removed from this house not fit to stay in. "Committed's" the word. Out I go! To Pass Christian and fam'ly at once, hat, coat, pocketbook, out, no return here!

CHARLIE: No, Mom! I'm putting Pop out! [*He has pushed Cornelius into the living room.*]

CORNELIUS: *Out by you never! —Whelp of—*

[*Bella has collected a variety of articles, none of which she called for above.*]

EMERSON [*ineffectually attempting restraint*]: Now, now, no, no, Bella. Awful weather outside.

BELLA: INSIDE WORSE!

CORNELIUS: *Hold onto her, Em! This will make us a scandal!*

[*Bella thrashes about for the door, knocking things over: her state of delirious passion stuns the men into immobilization. She somehow locates the door and throws it open to driving rain. There is the sound of an approaching car.*]

STACEY [*from upstairs*]: *Charlie, is something going on down there?!*

[*Bella has staggered out the front door.*]

BELLA [*from outside*]: *Stop, stop, cab! Here! Stop!*

[*There is a loud screech of brakes, etc. Charlie rushes out. Cornelius hobbles after him. The door is blown shut. Alone in the living room, Emerson moves about in confusion 'til his attention is focused on the appearance of Charlie's girlfriend, Stacey. She has descended to the landing, holding before her a large and fantastic beach towel that shields her body from view from shoulders to knees. The faded towel is patterned with beautiful, stylized creatures of the sea: fan-tail fish of many colors, sea-horses, crustaceans, shells, etc. Her face has an ingenuous wide-eyed charm.*]

STACEY [*in a deep Southern accent*]: Sounded like a disturbance goin' on down here.

BLACK OUT—INTERMISSION

ACT TWO

There is no passage of time.

STACEY [*in a deep Southern accent*]: Sounded like a disturbance goin' on down here.

EMERSON: Yes, a disturbance, now over. Come on down, little lady.

STACEY: My clothes are drainched, the upstairs is litterly flooded. —Has this house been unoccupied for a long time, Mistuh—McCorkle?

EMERSON: Naw, just neglected, honey, and I am not McCorkle. You see, Cornelius McCorkle who just went out for a while, he cares about nothing but what he imagines to be a political career.

STACEY: Charlie, is Charlie out, too?

EMERSON: Yeah, temporarily, honey. You are safely with me, an old Lodge brother of Corney's.

STACEY: Cain't locate my suitcase with dry things in it. Think it was left downstairs. Charles knows where but don't seem to hear when I call.

EMERSON: Ho, ho, Charlie is Charlie. Corney and wife just returned here from a funeral in Memphis which is responsible for the disturbance you heard.

STACEY: Aw. Charlie said nothing of it. Who died? Someone important?

EMERSON: Everyone is important, but some more than others. [*He advances to foot of stairs and extends his hand.*] Allow me to interduce myself to you, honey. I'm Emerson Sykes. You've probably heard of my enterprises known as Sykes and Sykes.

STACEY: No, suh—nothing.

EMERSON: Surprised to hear you haven't since I'm known statewide as the most prominent corporation head on the Gulf Coast, I assure you. [*His voice is quivering with the hunger that possesses some of the elderly for the young and lovely.*]

STACEY [*looking about from the landing*]: —Oh . . .

[*Emerson mounts one step.*]

EMERSON: Are you int'rested in employment in this area, honey?

STACEY: No, suh, not at present.

EMERSON: Then what is your present interest here on the Gulf Coast?

STACEY: Mr. Sykesand, I come here with Charlie McCorkle who is my only interest.

EMERSON: Oh, now, Charlie. No young lady's int'rest could be exclusively Charlie's.

STACEY: Will you kindly remain downstairs and locate Charlie. *Tell* him I must have my suitcase.

EMERSON: Tell me where you left it and I will bring it up to you, *baby*.

STACEY: Mr. Sykesand, you are too free with expressions like honey and baby. I want Charlie and Charlie only to bring my suitcase up here, nobody else. [*She calls out.*] CHARLIE, CHARLIE!

EMERSON: What is your name, young lady?

STACEY: Never mind. Just get Charlie.

EMERSON [*mounting another step*]: Charlie is out because of the disturbance and him being out, I think you ought to know of his reputation around here. You understand what I mean when I tell you that Charlie's notorious in Pascagoula as the local young stud? Shiftless of character, honey, unable or not willing to hold down a job?

STACEY: Charlie held down a job a good while in Yazoo City.

EMERSON: A job he got through family connections.

STACEY: I don't like the way you talk of him. You appear to be drunk and you got the shakes, which I can see by your hands and hear by your voice.

EMERSON: Sweetheart, I'm just reacting to the excitement of your—beautiful—presence—up there . . . [*He puts one foot a step higher.*] Oh, I know my appearance ain't youthful, but you'd be amazed at my fitness. Medical science provides a man my age with the vigor of youth plus the more appreciative and responsible attitude that comes with time and experience, yais, for instance, I take a thing by injection called depo-testosterone once or twice weekly along with one thousands units daily of vitamin E—to keep my virility up.

STACEY: Now, why would you imagine I'd be int'rested in such details as that?

EMERSON: I realize your infatuation with Charlie, you're drawn to the young. But, honey, look in his wallet and if it contains as much as a ten dollar bill, I would be surprised. —Now, can you see the denomination of the bill I just removed from my pocket? A century note, one hundred dollars, never step outa my house without one in my pocket just in case I should happen to run into a beautiful young lady in reduced circumstances like you brought here by Charlie.

STACEY: *This sounds like you are mistaking me for a whore! Don't you dare to climb up one step higher or I will—*

[*Emerson is seized by a slight cardiac attack. He staggers down the steps, fumbling in his pocket for nitro-glycerin tablets. He spills them, then falls to knees to recover a tablet, puts it in his mouth and washes it down with beer.*]

STACEY: *There! There! You've got a seizure, awful, pitiful, you better call for a doctor!* Charlie! Charlie!

[*The door opens. Wildly disheveled, suggesting an element of nature, Bella staggers in. Gasping for breath: her clothes are wet and mud-stained, a knee is bandaged. Charlie follows—slams and bolts door.*]

STACEY: *Charlie!*

[*Charlie catches Bella as she is about to collide with a chair. He shepherds her into the dining room. Stacey goes back up around the corner of the second landing.*]

CHARLIE: Set down till— [*He gets her into a dining room chair.*]

BELLA: Can't bend this knee, son.

CHARLIE: Better use another chair to support the laig you injured. [*He raises injured leg to the seat of another chair.*] Now just rest like that while I unfold that old cot of Hattie's in the kitchen.

BELLA: —Hattie not been around lately.

CHARLIE: Naw, been gone a long time, but I got her cot in the kitchen for you to lie down on.

BELLA: Lie down? No. No, I sleep sitting up. Oh, I—musta hurt my knee.

CHARLIE: Yeh, but the truck didn't hit you. And Dr. Crane was home, he bandaged your knee.

BELLA: Yes, he—

CHARLIE: He speaks highly of you, Mom. Said to me your mother's a great-hearted woman and that if Pop ever threatens again to put you away, he will put away Pop with support of entire community.

STACEY [*from upstairs, loudly*]: Charlie!

CHARLIE: Comin' honey. Mom had a little accident on the street. [*Then, to Bella.*] Now just rest, Mom. Pop's locked outa the house.

STACEY [*from above*]: My suitcase, Charlie.

CHARLIE: Yeh, yeh, got it. [*He rushes upstairs with it.*]

[*There is loud banging at the front door.*]

CORNELIUS [*from outside*]: Somebody open the door of this house for me, goddamn it.

EMERSON [*a hand to his chest*]: You outside still, Corney?

CORNELIUS [*from outside*]: Would I ask to get in if I wasn't!

[Emerson admits Cornelius who looks like an outraged and bedraggled old monster. There is a pause.]

EMERSON: Sorry, I—didn't know you—had a accident out there.

CORNELIUS: WHO? BOLTED? DOOR ON ME? HOLY GOD!

[*Emerson supports Cornelius feebly to his overstuffed chair and opens a beer for him. Cornelius slobbers the beer and chokes on it a bit.*]

CORNELIUS: Bella fell—forced a truck off highway to—avoid—hitting . . . her . . .

[*There is a crash of thunder. The lights go out for a couple of moments.*]

CORNELIUS: —Power? Failure? —Where's Bella?

EMERSON: In the dining room. —Sitting.

CORNELIUS: Reckon you could help me with this chair. Under a leak.

[*Emerson is collecting spilled nitro tablets—he ignores the question.*]

CORNELIUS [*moving his chair*]: Awlright. Just put a pail under it or the room'll be flooded.

[*Emerson ignores the suggestion.*]

CORNELIUS: Let it go, let it come down. [*To the audience.*] —Sinister these times. —East—West—armed to the teeth. —Nukes and neutrons. —Invested so much in every type of munitions, yes, even in germs, cain't afford not to use them, fight it out to the death of every human inhabitant of the earth if not the planet's destruction—opposed by no one . . .

EMERSON [*indifferently*]: No shit.

CORNELIUS [*to audience*]: I noticed a piece yesterday in the *Times-Picayune* infawming us that a—how'd it go?

EMERSON: Yes.

CORNELIUS: Unusual storm of rays indicate there's been a mysterious catastrophe somewhere in space . . .

EMERSON: Somewhere.

CORNELIUS: Em, are you mentally present? You seem distracted by something.

EMERSON: Need to pee, but Charlie's got him a bad-tempered woman up there.

CORNELIUS: Then go in the yard.

EMERSON: Raining.

CORNELIUS: Then use one of the buckets—unless you sit down to pee.

EMERSON: Then I'll go upstairs. [*Then loudly.*] She better stay outa my way. [*He mounts the stairs slowly.*]

STACEY [*from upstairs*]: Remain where you are till I have locked my door, Mr. Sykesand!

EMERSON [*responding to Stacey*]: I hope to avoid any second encounter between us. Lock your door before I go to the bathroom.

[*We hear a bolt slamming into place. Emerson continues above the landing.*]

CORNELIUS [*to audience*]: —Confusion? —Yais. —Common experience begins to confuse and bewilder . . . [*The phone rings.*] Will somebody answer that phone? Ringing after midnight! —No? —Well, fuck it. [*Picks up the phone.*] McCorkle residence . . . Still here, yes, gone up to the bathroom . . . confused? Yes, very, shocking state of confusion . . . you want to hear and observe? . . . Why not at his house or your whatever, why here tonight in my house? . . . Hmmm . . . Highly irregular procedure. Hmmm—*Now*? *Here now*? All right.

EMERSON [*upstairs*]: *Corney, no lights up here in the toilet . . . Jesus*!

CORNELIUS [*hanging up*]: . . . Christ . . . [*To the audience.*] Mortgaged property owned joint by him and that bitch Jessie—I reckon that fixed his wagon . . . well . . . I want no involvement, nope, not involved in it, no way . . .

[*There is a knock at door.*]

CORNELIUS: There's somebody at the door, but I am not going to it. *I said there is somebody at the door*!

CHARLIE [*entering*]: How'd you git back in here?

CORNELIUS: This is my house, nobody is locking me out!

[*Charlie goes to door and opens it.*]

CORNELIUS: Better now, Bella?

BELLA [*from the dining room*]: Stay out!

[*Two men enter. Charlie closes the door behind them and returns to the dining room.*]

CORNELIUS: You gentlemen are from . . .?

FIRST MAN: Foley's

SECOND MAN: Sorry to disturb you but we have been instructed to observe Mr. Sykes a short while before we remove him.

CORNELIUS: He has gone up to the bathroom a minute. Why don't you wait for him in there? —I want no involvement in this . . .

[*The men cross into the dining room.*]

CHARLIE: Mom, lean on my shoulder. We better go in the kitchen.

BELLA: It's here somewhere.

CHARLIE: What, Mom?

BELLA: Did I tell you? . . . no. But I told Chips—it's in this house. Must try to recollect . . .

[*Bella and Charlie go into the kitchen. There is a thunder clap. Emerson appears on the stair landing.*]

EMERSON: I tellya, Corney, conditions upstairs are . . .

CORNELIUS: No worse than down.

EMERSON: Think I better be going.

CORNELIUS: Wait'll the rain lets up . . . have another beer . . .

EMERSON: No thanks.

[*Emerson takes a beer.*]

CORNELIUS: Your house is dark. Jessie's still out with your key.

[*Thunder is heard and the lights flicker.*]

CORNELIUS: Power plant—lacks power. —Em?

EMERSON: Huh?

CORNELIUS: Tell me more about that old enterprise of yours, the Sykes and Sykes Refinery. I still don't know what they refined. Escapes my understanding.

EMERSON [*relaxing with his beer*]: Aw, that's on the back burner, what's cooking now is my upcoming chain of motels, first already under construction in Gulfport.

CORNELIUS: Upcoming?

EMERSON: Nite-A-Glory motel chain.

CORNELIUS: What was that you called it?

EMERSON: Nite-A-Glory.

CORNELIUS: Very suggestive title but—no criticism. Your business.

EMERSON: Last week I ordered the installation of them little ice chests, you know, one in each room. Also ordered the installation of vibrating mattresses for it.

CORNELIUS: Vibrate? Do they? Mattresses? Vibrate?

EMERSON: It works like this. You drop fifty cents in a slot and the mattress starts to vibrate.

CORNELIUS: Well I never. Meant to make the patrons believe they're out to sea on a cruise-ship?

EMERSON: Heh, heh, no! Of course some of the guests, the highway tourists, are old and tired. What they want is a soothing massage that's conducive to a quick and deep sleep. But the other couples, young ones, well they like the stimulating effect of the vibration at night.

CORNELIUS: Aw. Aw. Mattresses designed to arouse carnal impulses, huh? On them not usually blessed by civil or church ceremony, that the idea back of it? [*He stares desolately out at the audience. He shakes his head and takes another swallow of beer.*] *Disposal unit!* —of waste . . .

[*Cornelius turns to Emerson. Emerson notices the men.*]

CORNELIUS: Ain't that about what it is, our time of life?

[*Emerson moves downstage to avoid the men's scrutiny.*]

EMERSON [*uneasily, in a frightened stage whisper*]: Don't I see a couple of men in the dark dining room?

CORNELIUS [*chuckling*]: Neighbors drop over to offer congratulations when you come home from a family funeral, Em.

EMERSON: Anyhow, don't understand why they don't come in and speak instead of standing there in the dark with no talk, not a word between 'em.

CORNELIUS: Where'd you say these men are?

EMERSON [*with gathering alarm*]: In there, in the dark dining room, standing completely silent.

CORNELIUS [*to lighten Emerson's tension*]: Like "silent partners," Em?

EMERSON: Shit, this is no joke. You know, 'em?

CORNELIUS: Never seen 'em before in my life.

EMERSON: You're not lookin' at them.

CORNELIUS: They're prob'ly friends of Charlie's.

EMERSON: Charlie ain't with 'em. Don't seem natural. Call Charlie. Ask him.

CORNELIUS: Charlie! HEY, CHARLIE!

[*Emerson back ups and puts his beer on the table.*]

CORNELIUS: There's a coupla strange young men in the dining room. Did you let 'em in? What's their business, who'd they wanta see, me about something?

CHARLIE [*sticking his head out of the kitchen*]: You? No, not you. They come to see Mr. Sykes about something.

EMERSON: CORNY, GIMME MY GUN!

CORNELIUS: I'm not about to place a gun in the hands of a man over-excited as you.

EMERSON: I want my gun, goddamn it!

CORNELIUS [*picking up shotgun*]: Relax, no sweat, I got you covered with it.

SECOND MAN: Mr. Sykes?

FIRST MAN: Mr. Emerson Sykes?

SECOND MAN: Would you step in here a minute.

EMERSON: What faw? I don't talk business after midnight in a neighbor's house.

FIRST MAN: This business can't wait.

EMERSON: Turn the lights on in there!

CORNELIUS: Bella left 'em on when we went to Memphis and they're burnt out.

EMERSON: Mighty peculiar. Open the kitchen door so I can see 'em, Charlie. Otherwise, I—

[*A dim and ominous glow appears in dining room.*]

EMERSON [*reluctantly advancing*]: If you're here about employment at the motel, it'll be weeks before I'm ready to accept more than applications on file.

SECOND MAN [*after Emerson enters dining room*]: Outside, Mr. Sykes.

EMERSON: Naw, naw, take your hands off me!

CORNELIUS: No violence, men. Mr. Sykes ain't well.

[*There is a struggle with a few ad-libs.*]

BELLA [*coming out of the kitchen with Charlie*]: Em, is that Em goin? Say hello to Jessie! You all—

[*The commotion subsides as Emerson is hustled out the kitchen door. The door slams shut. Bella sits at the dining room table.*]

CHARLIE: I thought you said Mr. Sykes was your best friend in the Moose Lodge.

CORNELIUS: A crook is a crook, Lodge brother or not. Obviously you are not aware that some people in this world have still got a respect for honesty and for— Hell, it wasn't my doin'. His wife had disclosed certain matters, mortgage of joint property.

CHARLIE: Could be she just wanted him out of the way for someone younger.

CORNELIUS: It's none of your business so keep your nose out of it, huh? That man was trying to swing a fraudulent deal to put up and operate something not much better than a string of bordellos. You'd natcherly find that morally admirable, Charlie. It's the Dancie blood in you.

CHARLIE: Goddamn it, if you ain't mean as a junk-yard dawg. Dancies, Dancies, Mom's folks and mine. Never let up on 'em. But tonight you quit it! *I've had it!*

[*There is a pause. Cornelius changes strategy.*]

CORNELIUS: You misunderstood me, Charlie. Will ya help your Mom in here?

CHARLIE: Naw. Won't. For you to disturb her again?

CORNELIUS: Bella!

BELLA [*from the dining room*]: Yes, Cornelius?

CORNELIUS: Bella, would you come in here for a quiet but serious talk?

CHARLIE: Stay there, Mom.

BELLA: 'Sall right, Chips. Go on up and rest after your long trip.

[*Bella walks to the sofa as Charlie goes up the stairs.*]

CORNELIUS: That's right. Set down here, Bella. —I hope you're feeling a little better now.

BELLA: Lots to do today. Laundry to dry. Many things neglected to catch up on.

CORNELIUS: Bella, in your condition, don't over-do. Don't want to alarm you but a blood-pressure up to 220 over whatever, well, it's time to set the house in order, to relieve your own mind.

BELLA: Have you got something you want to say to me or not?

CORNELIUS: No. —But something to ask you.

BELLA: What've you got to ask me?

CORNELIUS: Off and on I've asked you this before, but now, you in your condition and me in mine and the roof of the house and every wall of the house threatening to collapse before *we* do, the question is too urgent *not* to call for an *immediate* answer.

BELLA: Question is—?

CORNELIUS: Concerning the Dancie money. It's time now you told me, don't you think so?

BELLA: —Dancie?

CORNELIUS [*leaning forward*]: Yes, Dancie.

BELLA: Money?

CORNELIUS: *Yes! Money!*

[*Cornelius stares at Bella silently.*]

CORNELIUS: Well, Bella?

BELLA: "Well, Bella" *what*?

CORNELIUS: WHERE IS THE DANCIE MONEY?

BELLA: My folks, the Dancies? Live on relief, you know that, why they're eating on food-stamps, got no money a-tall! Never heard of any Dancie money, no time ever!

CORNELIUS: Everyone else has heard of it, why folks that never heard of the notorious Dancies have heard of the Dancie money. And you deny it. Claim you never even heard it *existed*?

BELLA: NEVER—HEARD—IT EXISTED!

CORNELIUS [*resorting to softer tactics*]: You do remember your Grandpa? His devotion to you? When he passed on at close to the century mark, he had a shotgun on his bed and wouldn't admit a person inside his bedroom door except you, not even the preacher, Bella. But you he did let in and you were alone in the room with him, Bella. That's common knowledge, ask any dawg in the street.

BELLA [*staggering backwards*]: Ask any dawg—not me. They, they, the Dancies, they *got none*!

CORNELIUS [*discarding all restraint*]: OH, NO, NOT NOW THEY AIN'T. WHY? WHY?

CHARLIE [*from the stair landing*]: DON'T HOLLER AT MOM LIKE THAT!

CORNELIUS [*to the audience*]: SHE'S GOT IT! [*To Bella.*] *YOU* GOT IT, THAT'S WHY!

[*Cornelius gets his cane. Bella begins to breathe loudly.*]

CHARLIE [*descending to the living room*]: Mom, go in the—kitchen.

CORNELIUS: NOW FOR THE LAST TIME TELL!

BELLA: Te-tell?

CORNELIUS: WHERE THE HELL YOU HID IT BECAUSE I SWEAR IF YOU DON'T THIS GODDAMN HOUSE, EVERY TIMBER AND EV'RY SHINGLE OF IT, IS GONNA FALL, YES, WILL COLLAPSE ON YOUR HAID, MINE, EVERY, ALL UNDER IT, IT IS NOT GONNA *STAND*!

[*Bella cries out in terror and staggers off to the kitchen where a crash is heard.*]

CHARLIE: WHY, YOU DISGUSTING, CHEAP OLE—

[*Cornelius, with raised cane, turns again toward Charlie. Charlie seizes the cane and hurls it away while simultaneously there is a clap of thunder. The interior goes black: a confusion of outcries and sounds are heard.*]

STACEY [*from upstairs*]: CHARLIE! CHARLIE! LIGHTS OFF!

CORNELIUS: CA-ANE!

CHARLIE: MOM? MOM?

STACEY [*from upstairs*]: BLACK, ALL BLACK!

CHARLIE: MINUTE, STACEY! MOM, STAY BACK! AND YOU, STAY BACK, DON'T COME NEAR HER!

[*There is an interval in the shouting with sounds of neighbor's voices and the heavy breath of fury in the house.*]

STACEY: CHARLIE, WHAT HAPPENED?

CHARLIE: NOTHIN' HONEY, POWER FAILURE FROM STORM.

STACEY: CANDLES, ANY CANDLES? [*Stacey is now on the stair-landing.*] LAWD! I AM CRAWLIN' DOWN STAIRS!

[*The lights come back on as power is restored. Reassured, Stacey stands and illuminates the landing with a smile, modestly clasping her hands over her belly, protuberant with late pregnancy.*]

CHARLIE: 'Sall right, now, Stacey!

[*Charlie is in possession of the cane. Cornelius is supporting himself by chair-back.*]

STACEY: Such a—such a disturbance. Crawled down here on my—

CHARLIE: It's okay now, honey.

[*There is a pause as she looks about.*]

STACEY: Well, then, INTERDUCE ME!

[*Her smile widens. Cornelius removes one pair of glasses, puts on another, his jaw falling open in astonishment.*]

CHARLIE [*nervously*]: Come on down here, Stacey, don't be shy.

STACEY: Charlie, don't you know me better'n that?

CORNELIUS: I known her better'n that before I seen her.

[*Stacey remains on landing to adjust her panty hose.*]

STACEY: My clo's are still drainched.

CHARLIE: We walked here from the bus station in the rain.

STACEY: I said, "Charlie, call us a cab," an' he said there wasn't a cab in the county. Is that the truth?

CORNELIUS: No. You want a cab?

STACEY: Aw, not now, we're here. Lucky I don't catch cold since I lent my raincoat to m'girlfriend Polly an' she left town with it, ha ha!

CHARLIE: I'll light the gas logs in the fire.

STACEY: Good, good. I'd appreciate that. [*Hitches her skirt up higher.*]

CORNELIUS: Tell her not to come down till she's completed dressing.

STACEY: My panty hose don't fit me right.

CORNELIUS [*to audience*]: Jesus.

STACEY: I never did like these things, preferred to wear regular garters but they're hard to get now, seem to've gone out of style."

[*Bella enters with a tray bearing a dry and frowsy-looking omelet.*]

BELLA: Here's eggs.

CHARLIE: Mom, this is Stacey.

BELLA [*to Stacey*]: Why, how d' you do. [*Noticing her distended abdomen.*] How'd you *do*! I thought you all might be hungry so I—

CHARLIE: Mom thinks everyone's hungry.

STACEY: Well, *I* happen to *be*. —Hello, Mom.

BELLA: Hello. What's your name, honey?

STACEY: Stacey, it's a family name they give me as a first name.

BELLA: Oh?! 'Sthat so? Why?

STACEY: It's a lo-oong, long story! You see my uncle—

CORNELIUS: Don't tell it right now! Had too much t'night here.

STACEY: Could I, could we—have something t'drink, Mom?

BELLA: Y'know we been up in Memphis for several days. I was gonna make you some cocoa but the milk's gone sour.

[*Charlie takes a pint bottle of whiskey out of his trench coat pocket.*]

BELLA [*gasping*]: No, no, not whiskey, son! Charlie's older brother just— [*She sobs.*]

CORNELIUS: —Terminal—alcoholism, at thirty-one!

STACEY: Let's talk about it tomorrow, not tonight.

CORNELIUS: I'm a believer in talkin' all things out that can be talked out as quick as possible, miss.

CHARLIE: Stacey.

CORNELIUS: Stacey what?

CHARLIE: T'morrow she is gonna be Stacey McCorkle.

CORNELIUS: *IS* she?!

CHARLIE: Bright and early tomorrow her last name will be mine.

BELLA: —Oh . . .

CORNELIUS: What d'ya make of that, Bella? Something or nothing?

BELLA [*unmistakably so*]: Oh, I'm delighted about that!

CHARLIE: Yes.

STACEY [*crying a little*]: Yes. So happy I could die! —Just dieee!

CHARLIE: Sit down, Mom.

BELLA: If I had something to rest my leg on, I could sit down better. Y'see I—

CHARLIE: Mom had a little accident on the street.

STACEY: Oh? What was that, Mom? Oh, you got your laig bandaged.

BELLA: Yes, by Doc Crane, he lives right across the street.

CORNELIUS: The truck driver was injured. Took down names and addresses and intends to sue.

CHARLIE: Aw, wasn't hurt hardly a-tall.

CORNELIUS: No, no, not killed. He drove a privately owned truck off the highway to avoid hitting Bella.

CHARLIE: When you drove her outa the house.

CORNELIUS: Me drove her out? I told you to stop her! The responsibility's hers and she'll have to foot the bill, all of it, man's injury, damage to his truck, oh, if it comes under five thousand she'll git off light.

STACEY: This is no time to discuss the cost of something that might of cost Mom's life. Lemme put something under. [*She puts a pillow on floor.*] Better now, Mom? Don't hurt much?

BELLA: No, no, I'll tell you something. A big hurt like we got up there in Memphis, it, it—sort of numbs you to anything else for a while.

CHARLIE: Doc Crane says nothing is broke. A miracle, he called it.

STACEY: A case of divine intervention. Well, Mom, you can depend on me to take care of the house till you're completely recovered, yais, and after. Charlie's told me how bad you need some assistance, and I am happy to give it. Only too happy.

[*Bella, forgetting her injury, attempts to stand.*]

BELLA: —Ow!

STACEY: Stay there, Mom. Did you want something?

BELLA: Yes, honey, Doc Crane give me some tablets for temporary relief of—sedation.

CHARLIE: He gave 'em to me. He said take two at once. —It slipped my mind. [*He removes them from his pocket.*]

STACEY: Better get her something to wash 'em down with.

[*Charlie crosses through the dining room.*]

CORNELIUS: Play your hand. See what it's worth in a courtroom.

[*Charlie goes into the kitchen. There is a pause.*]

STACEY: Don't you worry, Mom. Just rest. [*She picks up the framed photograph of Chips on an incidental table.*] —Is this—?

BELLA: Honey, that was my first-bawn. —Chips . . .

STACEY: Very good looking young man. Charlie has told me about his brother Chips, Mom, I known a lot of boys like him. I unnerstood and I liked 'em. They used to flock into The Late and Lively, where I was employed as a waitress befo' my engagement to Charlie, yais, boys like this come in there when the bars closed for our ninety-nine cent breakfast of aigs, sausage, grits and biscuits, haws-biscuits with sawmill gravy and with chicory coffee.

[*Charlie enters with water for Bella.*]

STACEY: —I made acquaintances with them—I sympathized with their problems. Oh, they had many problems. I always advised the couples to stick together, to settle, make homes together. Such boys are not understood by society, Mom. I think they are persecuted by society, Mom. Thrown out of jobs. Beat up. Despised for difference they can no more help than they could help being born. Human. With talents. But society—Well, you heard of Anita Bryant. Just one of many. And sometimes, often—I did bring some to Jesus! You see, Mom, I'm a bawn-again Christian.

BELLA: What is that?

CHARLIE: Stacey's a bawn-again Christian.

STACEY: *Saved by my Savior, by His blessed forgiveness! Many, many times saved from temptations of Satan!* [*Her voice rises rhapsodically.*] *Came to Him and He saved me, from falling, falling! I fall to my knees before the throne of my Lord and Savior!* Mom, Mom, fall to *Him with me!*

[*The following five lines overlap each other.*]

CHARLIE: Stacey, Mom's had a—

STACEY: *Blessed, oh, Blessed! Defender of us from evil!*

CHARLIE: Accident on the—

STACEY: Mom, kneel with me!

CHARLIE: Don't excite her!

STACEY [*beside herself*]: Let's pray for peace in this house which is attacked by demons! All together, pray with me! WE ARE LOST LITTLE SHEEP, ERRED AND STRAYED FROM THY WAYS,

BROKEN YOUR HOLY COMMANDMENTS, ENGAGED IN FORNICATION. HAVE MERCY UPON US THAT YIELDED TO THE TEMPTATIONS OF THE FLESH, YES, JESUS, WE IMPLORE THY FORGIVENESS! THY DIVINE MERCY, CHRIST! MAKE US FIT FOR SALVATION! DESERVING OF LIFE ETERNAL, LAWD, LAWD, SHOW US THE WAYYYYYY!

CORNELIUS: Shudderup, goddamn it!

BELLA: Honey, let's pray QUIETLY together.

CHARLIE [*kneeling with Stacey*]: Stacey, Mom says quietly.

BELLA: It don't have to be quite so loud!

STACEY: OH, IT IS COMIN' ON ME! WAIT, IT'S COMING, I FEEL IT, THE GIFT OF TONGUES! WHAHOOOOOOO! BE-BE, YAIS, BAH! OH, BLESSED! BE, BE, BE, BE, LIEVE! ALL, ALL, ALL COME FORTH! BAH! BOW! WALLAH, YAIS WALLAH! SALVAREDEMPTION IN ME, DEEP, DEEP SALVAREDEMPTION, GLORY IN ME, AH, GLORY, GO DEEP IN ME IN GLORY, AH, AH, GAH, WALLAH, WOMB! WOMB! WOMB . . . [*As if arrived at orgasm, she falls back onto the carpet.*]

BELLA: Charlie, I think she's in labor, hope she don't drop the baby. Excuse me, honey. [*She steps over Stacey.*] Call the hospital for her.

CORNELIUS [*at the phone*]: I'm callin' the POLICE!

BELLA: Wha's that man say, Charlie?

CORNELIUS: POLICE! QUICK! TWENTY SEVEN SOUTH ELM!

[*There are no further sounds from Stacey as she lies as if in post-orgasmic exhaustion. Charlie wrests phone from Cornelius.*]

CHARLIE: Police? Ignore that call! Cornelius McCorkle is— [*He jiggles the hook.*]

CORNELIUS: Is *what*? Say it. I want to hear it!

CHARLIE: *Vicious, crazy ole man!*

CORNELIUS: Said it! —Confounded—!

CHARLIE: Destroyed a son, a daughter! Persecuted us all!

STACEY: Amen.

[*A relative quiet descends. Stacey lies spread-eagled on her back.*]

CHARLIE: —Stacey, can you get up?

STACEY [*moans*]: Nooo.

BELLA: How long is she been—?

CHARLIE: Seven months. Or more.

BELLA: I better make her some cocoa.

CHARLIE: You said the milk's sour, Mom.

BELLA [*inspired*]: Call the Moose Lodge and ask for someone to come over. Several if—

CHARLIE: The police had hung up before! —

BELLA: The Moose Lodge will come over.

[*The soft yap and scratch at the door of the dog, Peppy, has gone unheeded. It pushes its way in and slinks warily to its basket. Stacey has noticed only the opening of the door. She is repossessed by rapture.*]

STACEY [*springing up, arms aloft*]: CHRIST COME IN THE DOOR! Enter this—

CHARLIE: Stacey, no, no.

STACEY: BLESSED SAVIOUR HAS VISITED THIS HOUSE!

CORNELIUS: Goddamn it!

[*Stacey rushes blindly toward the audience. Charlie clutches her just before she falls off the stage.*]

BELLA: Hold on to her, son.

CHARLIE: Tryin' t' hold her, Mom.

BELLA: Careful, don't hurt the baby!

[*Charlie wrestles her to the carpet and straddles her swollen belly. From outside, there is the sound of a car approaching, screeching to a halt in front of the house. A car door slams. This activates Cornelius. He stumbles over Charlie and Stacey in his arthritic charge out the door.*]

CORNELIUS: Officer! Officer!

OFFICER [*from outside*]: Okay. What's goin' on?

BELLA: It was all a mistake, everything is all right here.

CORNELIUS [*from outside*]: Yais, I'll tell you the problem! We'd just got back from a fam'ly fun'ral in Memphis when we discover the other one, Charlie, had brought a pregnant lunatic here in our absence, that's the—

[*Charlie charges out. The following lines take place outside.*]

CHARLIE [*from outside*]: Wait a minute! That ain't the problem a-tall, I'll tell you the problem! This sick, crazy ole—

CORNELIUS [*from outside*]: You goddamn whelp with your whore. Intends to marry a pregnant demented prostitute in the—

STACEY: I'm comin' to you, Jesus. [*She goes out the front door.*]

CHARLIE [*from outside*]: He's talkin' about my fiansay who was respectably employed at—

SECOND OFFICER [*from outside*]: Awright, all in the car, can't wake up the whole neighborhood.

CORNELIUS [*from outside*]: Look here! I'm Cornelius McCorkle, candidate for congress in this district!

OFFICER [*from outside*]: Yeh, yeh, get your names at the station.

CORNELIUS [*from outside*]: Be goddamned if I get in a police car with a Jesus-freak of a whore!

CHARLIE [*from outside*]: SAID THAT TOO OFTEN!

[*There is a blow and Cornelius' yell of pain.*]

OFFICER [*from outside*]: Let's get out a here before—

CORNELIUS [*from outside*]: *Broke my dentures!*

SECOND OFFICER [*from outside*]: Before he files claims against my friend Charlie here, why don't we stop by the Moose Lodge. My Dad's there tonight. This thing can all be—

FIRST OFFICER [*from outside*]: Awright, Pee Wee, the Moose Lodge first, okay, okay.

STACEY [*from outside*]: Keep praying! Pray! Jesussss!

[*Sounds subside with the departing squad car. During the entire scene outside, Bella has executed a slow, bemused and tottering return to sofa. For a few moments she sits there as if senseless. Then her eyes focus on a small bottle of sedative pills that were given to her by Dr. Crane after she fell on the street. She lurches forward to remove it from the low table that fronts the sofa. Clumsily and exhaustedly she gets it open and spills the contents on the table. She collects several pills and puts them in her mouth, is unable to swallow but notices a beer bottle on the table and washes the pills down with beer.*]

BELLA: Mmmmm . . .. [*Apparently the beverage hasn't displeased her. she takes several more swallows. A synergistic reaction occurs. Gradually the apparition of Chips becomes visible behind the transparency of the dining room. The apparition stands motionless for a while before Bella lifts her clear, deeply innocent eyes to him.*] Oh, son, Chips! [*She attempts to rise unsuccessfully.*] Where've you been so long, such a—

[*The apparition never speaks, but his recorded voice is projected over speakers.*]

APPARITION OF CHIPS: Clock.

[*There is a pause as she tries again to get up.*]

APPARITION OF CHIPS: Clock.

[*Delicate music is heard.*]

BELLA: —Long, long time, ohh, I—

APPARITION OF CHIPS: Clock.

BELLA: Long trip back . . .

APPARITION OF CHIPS: Clock. Clock. Clock.

[*With a slow, dance-like motion the apparition of Chips turns and the light behind the transparency dims out. Pause. A soft cacophony of late highway street sounds is heard. Bella draws a deep breath and staggers to the hat rack by the front entrance. She fumbles a large envelope out of her bag.*]

BELLA: Terrible storm. Little Joanie.

[*There is a knock at door and it swings open. Jessie enters.*]

JESSIE: Bella, it's me, Jessie.

BELLA: Yes.

JESSIE: Dr. Crane said he thought you might be alone here and he suggested I come over and see how you are. What a night this has been! You took a fall on the street, nearly run down by a truck? Oh, Bella, and your door was unlocked with that sex-fiend still at large on the Gulf Coast highway. [*She hangs her transparent raincoat on the hat-rack. She is attired in a frilly pastel negligee.*] Emerson Sykes removed to Foley's, was it violent, Bella, did he put up a fight?

BELLA: Emerson? Was here, but I think he left now.

JESSIE [*to audience*]: The situation between us had come to a head, no longer tolerable. His removal to a closed ward at Foley's was all that was left to do.

BELLA: What? What?

JESSIE [*to Bella*]: Never mind— [*She touches Bella's forehead.*] —Fever? I think a little. Ahhh . . . . [*To the audience.*] What a lot we've been through! With probably more to come . . . [*To Bella.*] —What's that envelope you're holding, Bella?

BELLA: Jessie, I got a letter from Little Joanie. You remember my Little Joanie?

JESSIE: Of course I do. Who could forget little Joanie?

BELLA: This letter was in the mailbox when we got back from Memphis. I pretended like it was just an advertisement. Or Cornelius would've torn it right up. Joanie's in a hospital, State Hospital Number Three.

JESSIE: Why, that's the—

BELLA: Lunatic asylum, I know. Uncle Archie has been there thirty years now.

JESSIE: How did this happen to Joanie?

BELLA: I don't know. I haven't opened the letter. Can't, just can't. I wonder if you would read it first and prepare me for it a little?

JESSIE: Bella, I've switched to contact lenses and have removed them for the night. Can't read without them. But give me the letter. I'm going to open it for you. You got to know the contents and the sooner the better.

[*She opens the letter and hands it to Bella.*]

BELLA: —Oh, my God!

JESSIE: Bad as that?

BELLA: There are—terrible details.

JESSIE: If you want my advice on how to handle the problem, you'd better read it to me.

BELLA: "Dear Mom, don't commit me. They can only hold me ten days without your permission or Pop's. He would give it I know, but I know you wouldn't. All I had was a little nervous break down after that sonovabitch I lived with in Jefferson Parish quit me and went back to his fucking wife." —Excuse me, Jessie, she seems to have picked up some very bad langwidge somehow.

JESSIE: Never mind, read it all. Nothing shocks me since Emerson started talking in his sleep.

BELLA: "That black motha, he quit me without a dime. Honestly, I was much better off at Miss Lottie's where I last was, would've gone back there but the place was shut down because Miss Lottie stopped paying off somebody to keep it open and it was election time. Well, Mom, I know you got lots of problems of your own. Cheer up. That's my philosophy always. I swear I'm okay, never felt better in my life, so if you get papers, refuse to sign them and say nothing about this to Pop. I'll get back on my feet, can either return to Miss Lottie's or get my old job back at the Pizza King on the highway. I know the manager can't wait to get me back there. So, don't let nothing upset you, things will work out for the best. Love, your little Joanie."

JESSIE: Yes, it contains some terrible details, but she does say she never felt better in her life. And that is probably because she's landed in the right place for her. There's no way you can conceal this from Cornelius. If they don't hear from you, they will get in touch with him—for humanity's sake. You forget it tonight. It's going to take care of itself, one way or another and—Oh! I guess I'd better check up on Emerson's admission to Foley's. Have you still got that phone on the landing Cornelius installed when he was running for Mayor with arthritis? [*Bella nods vaguely. Jessie goes to stair landing. The phone call is audible.*] Operator, would you please connect me with the Horace Dean residence? Mary Louise, this is a night to remember! Emerson Sykes is hauled off to a nursing home under restraint. Two men required. It happened here at the McCorkles', apparently he put up a terrible fight and will continue to do so. No chance, no way, in to stay! We'll discuss it later. Must lower my voice. —Poor Bella's received a letter from the State asylum and it comes from her daughter that she calls "Little Joanie," and little Joanie is in the state bin, sitting, and claims she never felt better in her life. [*She cackles.*] Isn't that a *riot*! [*There is a loud knock at door.*] Somebody's at the door. I've got to see who—talk later . . . [*Jessie descends from the landing, calling out in her social voice—*] Who is there please?

MALE VOICE: Officer, ma'am.

JESSIE [*hoarse whisper, fluffing out hair*]: That's a dead give-away, no name, just "Officer, ma'am"? Who's fooling whom? [*To the audience.*] Mary Louise Dean's niece claims that she was assaulted when she answered the door after dark alone in the house. Says she admitted this attractive young man, well-dressed and polite as pie, till all of a sudden . . . [*She makes a growling noise.*] Of course, Mary Louis likes to embellish a story, and as for the niece, a bleached blond from Tuscaloosa, well, there's contradictory rumors.

[*The knocking at the door has continued.*]

JESSIE [*to audience*]: Whoever you are at the door, identify yourself, please. Knocks at the door are not an identification.

MALE VOICE: Police officer, ma'am.

JESSIE [*to audience*]: Maybe so, maybe not so. [*She goes to the door.*] Who's there please?

MALE VOICE: Officer Jackson.

JESSIE: Here on what business, hammering on the door?

MALE VOICE: To check on a disturbance reported in the home of Mr. Cornelius McCorkle. Deposition from Mrs. McCorkle is needed before we can file a complaint, ma'am.

JESSIE: I really don't know what you're talking about.

BELLA [*loudly*]: What is it, Jessie?

MALE VOICE: Mrs. McCorkle, is that Mrs. McCorkle?

JESSIE [*attaching the door chain*]: Bella, let me handle this. This is not a matter for you to get involved in.

MALE VOICE: I got to speak to the lady of the house.

JESSIE: May we see your credentials? Otherwise the door is going to stay latched. Just show your credentials, if any.

MALE VOICE: Can you see this badge?

JESSIE: I'm not going to look out there and get a gun stuck in my face and neither is Mrs. McCorkle. You hear my voice and I hear yours, so just ask Mrs. McCorkle if she's got anything to say about what happened here. I wasn't personally present, not in the residence and not on the street. I was having my rose garden bath. But Mrs. McCorkle was. However, I'm not sure she is in a condition to make what you call a—what? A what did you call it?

MALE VOICE: Deposition.

JESSIE: What shall I say, Bella?

MALE VOICE: Goddamn it! I've *got* to talk to Mrs. McCorkle. [*He puts his foot in the door.*]

JESSIE: Profanity is not called for. Stop holding door open!

MALE VOICE: Just a crack so she can talk to me through it, because otherwise, Charlie McCorkle's ass is going to be in a sling.

JESSIE: How dare you talk like that! No police officer would express himself to ladies in such language!

MALE VOICE: Mrs. McCorkle!

JESSIE: Bella, say you know nothing!

BELLA: Know? —Nothing. Just a terrible stawm.

JESSIE: Did you hear that? She said she knows nothing except a terrible stawm. That's exactly what she said to me. A terrible storm blew the door open and everybody went out.

MALE VOICE: Ladies, I'm sorry but if you want to help Charlie, I'm a good friend of Charlie's, Mrs. McCorkle knows that. You tell her I am Police Lieutenant Bruce Lee Jackson. Was called Pee Wee at school, she probably just knows me as Pee Wee Jackson, who want to school with Charlie.

BELLA: Did he say Pee Wee Jackson? Little Pee Wee Jackson? Invite him in, he's probably cold and hungry.

JESSIE [*unlatching and opening door*]: You should have identified yourself in the first place.

[*The Officer enters wearing a mackintosh.*]

JESSIE: Oh. —Allow me to—

[*He removes hat and gives it to Jessie. The name Pee Wee is hardly suitable to his present stature and appearance. He is handsome and strapping. Jessie is impressed and there is now a touch of coquetry in her manner.*]

JESSIE: Excuse the way I'm—not dressed. We were so alarmed when you knocked. I mean I was. Bella hasn't heard about the rapist. —Surely they don't call you Pee Wee anymore.

OFFICER JACKSON [*crossing to the sofa.*]: No, they don't anymore. Now, Miss McCorkle, I know you don't want Charlie put in jail by your husband.

JESSIE: It would be totally unsuitable now. Surely they call you—didn't you say Bruce? Bruce Lee?

OFFICER JACKSON: Excuse me. I can see that Mizz McCorkle's not feeling good but I do have to try to get her to make a statement, or otherwise, Mizz McCorkle, that's just what's gonna happen, your husband— [*He speaks slowly, leaning toward Bella.*] Your husband, Cornelius McCorkle, I don't want to speak against him to you, Ma'am, but he's always had a reputation for being rough on his children.

BELLA [*nods slowly with a sad look*]: —Children. Three!

OFFICER JACKSON: Yes, all three.

BELLA: Three—yes, three . . .

OFFICER JACKSON: I drove Charlie and the ole man to the Moose Lodge but he insists, now, that his son Charlie be put under arrest and he keeps making awful remarks about your folks. Hate to tell you so but he won't let up on the subject of your folks and those being the circumstances, I'm sure you'll be glad to say that if Charlie hit Mr. McCorkle it was in self-defense and in defense of his wife. Huh? Understand, Mizz McCorkle?

JESSIE: —Well, as you see, Bella is not in a condition to make a statement right now.

BELLA [*to audience*]: Cornelius McCorkle's only int'rest is money to run for office . . .

OFFICER: Mizz McCorkle just *made* a statement and I am taking it down.

BELLA: Chips, you remember Chips?

OFFICER: Yes, Ma'am, but—

BELLA: And Joanie? Little Joanie? Little Joanie and Chips and Charlie?

OFFICER: Charlie best, Mizz McCorkle. We double-date a lot and he wants me to stand up for him at his wedding tomorrow.

BELLA: You knew little Joanie?

OFFICER: Yes, she was very well known, a very well-known girl.

JESSIE [*firmly*]: Officer, may I speak with you privately at the door?

OFFICER: Excuse me, no time, must hurry back to the Lodge with this deposition, g'night, ladies. [*He exits.*]

JESSIE: You come back. Anytime. [*She moves downstage and delivers an "interior monologue" to the audience.*] What a handsome and sexy, what a strapping young man that boy we used to call Pee Wee has grown into. Now that the children are grown and gone away, I see nothing wrong in looking at attractive and vigorous young men such as Bruce Lee Jackson or Spud, that young Irish waiter at the Dock House. [*To the audience.*] Do you? I always give Spud a good up and down look and since my rejuvenation, he returns it, and, of course, I slip him an extra tip as I leave . . . I'm sort of put out with Mary Louise Dean that she's had him first, but then she had her rejuvenation first, too. —I didn't have mine till I saw how hers turned out. —Miracle.

BELLA: Chips stood right there in the dining room and said just one word to me. He said, "clock," yes. Why would he say "clock"? —

JESSIE [*turning from the audience*]: —Bella, you seem to feel better, but I think you ought to sleep downstairs tonight, in case of a setback. —Dr. Crane is home. Told me it was providential that the accident hadn't been fatal. [*She gives Bella a pat on the shoulders.*] —Of course, sooner or later something always is—but, if I had to make a bet on you outlasting this house, I think I'd make it. —Tomorrow I'm going to talk seriously to you about the condition of this house—deplorable—won't stand . . . Ouu—waterbug! No wonder.

BELLA: I don't hate Cornelius, but I just won't let him put me away till all three children are back. —This house having been built with Dancie money is theirs, their home. "Clock?" —Why would he say "clock?" [*She touches her lips.*]

JESSIE [*returning to address the audience*]: No matter how much younger I look by virtue of surgery at Ochsner's, I know my age. However! —I think I have a right to lie about it. Don't you?

[*Bella puts her head down.*]

JESSIE: It is a forgivable, understandable sort of deception in a woman with my—sometimes I think almost unnatural attraction to—desire for—sex with young men . . . Spud at the Dock House, he understands the looks I give him and the large tips, he knows what for—expectation! [*She lowers her voice confidingly as she continues speaking to the audience.*] He knows my name, address and phone number! —and so does Mr. Black—that's what I call death . . . Oh, I didn't give it to him, but of course he knows it. Everyone's address is jotted down in his black book but some for earlier reference than others. Still, I refuse to take cortisone till the pain's past bearing, since it swells up the face which would undo the pain and expense of all those lifts at Ochsner's . . .

BELLA: "Clock." [*She nods with understanding.*] Jessie, help me up off the sofa.

JESSIE: You want to go to the ladies room?

BELLA: I want to go to the clock.

JESSIE: —I can give you the time.

BELLA: It's not what I want from the clock.

JESSIE: What else can you get from the clock.

BELLA: This clock is different.

JESSIE: Yes, it's run down, it's stopped. Want me to set and wind it for you, Bella?

BELLA: No, just help me get it down from the mantel, please.

JESSIE: It bothers you, does it? I know some people are allergic to clocks. Reminds them of time passing too fast . . .

BELLA: For me, time's about finished but I got children, Jessie, and a gran'chile expected. Family got to continue. Can't just go. —I reckon you've heard of the Dancie money, Jessie.

JESSIE: Why, yes, it's legendary but doesn't seem to exist.

BELLA: It exists, and I got it. My grannie gave it to Granpa and Granpa gave it to me the day he died. I was alone with him, Jessie. He took the Dancie money out of his pocket where he'd kept a tight hold on it years and years. Said to me: "Bella, take this money and hide it, I'm going now—g'bye."

JESSIE: —Why, my God! —How much money is it?

BELLA: More than I would like Mary Louise Dean to know.

JESSIE: What makes you think I'd—tell her.

BELLA: Ev'rybody's got a weakness, Jessie, like I got eating and you got Mary Louise.

JESSIE: Bella, suspicion is a disease.

BELLA: Is it? Well, I got it. And I got the Dancie money back of that clock. Don't stand there asking me how much. Never mind how much. Back of that clock.

[*Jessie has joined Bella by the mantel clock, she turns it around.*]

JESSIE: There's nothing back of it, Bella.

BELLA: Back of it opens and a envelope's inside it.

JESSIE: *Ohhhhh*! Opens, does it, I *seeee*!

BELLA: Lemme, lemme, I know this clock was Grannie Dancie's! [*She opens it and removes thick yellowed envelope.*]

JESSIE: That envelope is disintegrating with age. I'll remove the money and put it in a fresh one.

BELLA [*holding tight to her envelope*]: No, no, no! —You don't!

JESSIE: Stop being so childish, Bella, you're talking to Jessie Sykes, not to Cornelius or—

BELLA: Yes, he wants it, too. I'll put it in my bag.

JESSIE [*snappishly*]: Where *is* your bag?

BELLA: Look around, you'll find it.

JESSIE: Oh, the bag.

[*Jessie turns and crosses to fetch the bag. With startling alacrity, Bella conceals the envelope under her arm. Jessie returns with the bag.*]

JESSIE: All right, the bag. Put the envelope in it. —You hear me, Bella?

BELLA: I hear a terrible stawm.

JESSIE: You'd better get back on the sofa. [*She helps Bella across the room.*] Sit down.

BELLA: Where?

JESSIE: On the sofa! Where else?

[*Bella falls onto the sofa, breathing hard.*]

JESSIE: Now give me the envelope.

BELLA: —Want a snack? From the ice-box in the kitchen?

JESSIE: No, no, certainly not, I'm on a low calorie diet and the contents of your "ice-box" would horrify Dr. Scarsdale. I want just that envelope containing the Dancie money. Where is it? Flown further south with the birds? [*Her voice is shrill, agitated.*]

BELLA: —I'm dying, Jessie. —Go get—Doctor . . .

JESSIE: Nonsense. You're putting on. And here's the envelope, under your arm. [*She snatches it.*] Look, I'm putting it your bag. [*She places the fat envelope in Bella's bag and holds the bag.*] Now.

BELLA: My bag is in your lap.

JESSIE: It couldn't possibly be in a safer place.

BELLA: I want my bag in *my* lap.

JESSIE: If you weren't sick, I would be outraged, Bella.

BELLA: I want my bag with the Dancie money in it here in my lap.

JESSIE: You are in no condition to care for it tonight.

[*Bella grabs the bag from Jessie's lap and hugs it fiercely against her.*]

BELLA: You got not children left. You don't know. —Jessie, why don't you go over to Mary Louise Dean's place since you got so much to tell her?

[*Jessie and Bella abruptly engage in a struggle for the bag.*]

BELLA: Ahhhh, ahhhh, ahhhh! [*She sprawls back as if lifeless on the sofa.*]

JESSIE [*seizing the bag*]: If rumors are right about it, the Dancie money's a fortune. [*She removes envelope from bag and stuffs it down her negligee.*] —There now, it's in a safe place. —I'll go get the doctor if not too late. [*She rushes to door. The moment she opens it she starts screaming histrionically as she runs outside.*]

BELLA: —Stawm! —Terrible. [*She rises to her feet with great difficulty. Ghostly outcries of children fade in—in Bella's memory—projected over house speakers with music under. She moves with slow, stately dignity into the dining room, which is lighted by light-spill from the living room. She will hold the stage until a plausible passage of time permits Jessie to return with Dr. Crane.*] —Children?

VOICE OF YOUNG CHIPS: —Mommy!

VOICE OF YOUNG CHARLIE: —Is supper ready?

VOICE OF YOUNG JOANIE: —Mommy calls us when to come in for supper.

VOICE OF YOUNG CHARLIE: —We can play hide and—

VOICE OF YOUNG CHIPS: —Fly, sheep, fly.

VOICE OF YOUNG JOANIE: —Let's catch fire flies!

VOICE OF YOUNG CHARLIE: —Yeh, yeh, let's catch fire-flies, lotsa fire-flies tonight.

[*Bella's slow, heavy breathing is heard as she fumbles about for the match-box on the table and lights the candelabra.*]

BELLA: —Hattie? Hattie? Oh, Hattie . . .

GHOSTLY BLACK VOICE: Yais, Mizz McCorkle?

BELLA: If supper is ready, call the children in, please. —Don't let them—chase—fire-flies, they—never—stop—chasing fire-flies . . .

DR. CRANE [*from outside*]: All right, Jessie, I told May to call an ambulance—

JESSIE [*from outside*]: From somewhere close, I hope.

[*Dr. Crane, a man in his mid-thirties, enters wearing a raincoat over pajamas, carrying a medicine kit, followed by Jessie.*]

DR. CRANE: Well, where *is* she, Jessie?

JESSIE: She had collapsed right there.

BELLA [*to audience*]: Won't—wait for—Cornelius, this is—Progress Club Night . . . Runnin' fo' Mayor? —Oh, Lawd . . .

JESSIE: Gracious, how did she—?

BELLA: Hattie? Did you hear me? Call them in, looks like rain . . .

[*Dr. Crane has entered the dining room and has taken hold of Bella's wrist.*]

JESSIE [*hovering near arch*]: How is her—?

DR. CRANE: Trying to find it. —Now. —Slow. —Not regular—Bella, can you hear me?

BELLA: Who is it?

DR. CRANE: It's Dr. Crane, Bella. Just dropped over to see that you're all right.

JESSIE: Should be removed soon as the ambulance gets here.

BELLA: 'sthat—Jessie Sykes—In there? She tried to grab my bag from me. Where is—?

DR. CRANE: What, Bella?

BELLA: My bag with the Dancie money.

JESSIE: What was that she asked for?

DR. CRANE: Her bag with the Dancie Money is what she said. The Dancie Money? Seem to remember hearing some talk about it years ago.

JESSIE: Nothing to it, just talk, a myth, a legend.

BELLA: My bag.

JESSIE: Her bag's on the sofa but contains nothing except every candy bar on the market.

BELLA: Bag.

DR. CRANE: Bring the bag in here, Jessie.

JESSIE [*fetching it*]: Here it is, you can see for yourself if you doubt my word about it.

DR. CRANE [*examining the contents of bag, pockets candy bars*]: Bella, the bag had nothing in it— [*Then, gently . . .*] but evidence that you disregard my instructions on diet. [*Pause.*]

[*Voices of Bella's children fade in faintly.*]

VOICE OF YOUNG CHIPS AND CHARLIE: —Five, six, pick up sticks!

VOICE OF YOUNG JOANIE: —Seven, eight, get them straight!

BELLA: Get it back from Jessie.

JESSIE: Why, how—*Outrageous*, I'm—*Speechless*!

[*The doctor notices a corner of the fat yellowed envelope protruding from top of Jessie's negligee.*]

DR. CRANE [*removing it from concealment*]: Excuse me, Jessie.

JESSIE: —Just all the—confusion, you know. You surely—

BELLA [*with a luminous smile*]: It's mine, not for Jessie, not for Cornelius—for *Charlie's—children—coming.*

[*Specters of young Chips, Charlie and Joanie enter and take their places around the table with Bella.*]

JESSIE: I remember now why I took it. Come here for a moment. Do you know how much there is of it? Much more than ever reported!

DR. CRANE: I will write down the precise amount when I've counted it.

JESSIE: In my presence as witness, for your protection.

DR. CRANE [*staring at her coldly*]: Why, yes, of course.

JESSIE: I could also get Mary Louise Dean. An amount like that—

[*Cries of the children fade in again.*]

VOICES OF YOUNG CHIPS, CHARLIE AND JOANIE [*together*]: —Olly, olly, oxen free!

DR. CRANE [*crossing through arch into dining room*]: Bella? Here is the Dancie money.

JESSIE: Mary Louise Dean has a strong box where it could be held—overnight . . .

[*The subjective cries have continued in varying tone and volume, enchanting with the lost lyricism of childhood.*]

VOICE OF YOUNG CHIPS: —*Dark*!

VOICE OF YOUNG CHARLIE: *Mommy*!

VOICE OF YOUNG JOANIE: We're *Hungry*!

JESSIE: I'm gonna sit and remain here till responsible witnesses are summoned.

BELLA: That chair is—little—Joanie's . . .

[*Dr. Crane firmly, almost forcibly draws Jessie to the living room.*]

JESSIE [*to audience*]: *Who in this world can be trusted?* [*To the doctor.*] Yes! I'm astonished at you, Dr. Crane.

DR. CRANE: You are not as astonished at me as I am at you, Jessie Sykes. Can't you see that the immediate concern is not with money?

BELLA: Chips, will you say—Grace . . .

GHOSTLY VOICE OF YOUNG CHIPS: Bless this food to our use and ourselves to Thy service.

BELLA AND HER CHILDREN: Amen.

BELLA [*faintly*]: Hattie? —You can start servin' now . . . [*Her head sinks slowly to the failing support of her hands.*]

JESSIE: As long as we've known each other to imply such a disgraceful thing is—

DR. CRANE: Jessie, I think you might dismiss that subject in the presence of death.

[*He completes the sentence by drawing his hand gently across Bella's eyes to close them. Ceremonially the ghostly children rise from the family table and slip soundlessly back into the dark, each turning at the kitchen door to glance back at their mother. A phrase of music is heard.*]

SLOW CURTAIN

SOURCES, NOTES, AND ACKNOWLEDGMENTS

SOURCES AND NOTES

Williams wrote at least eight drafts of what eventually became *A House Not Meant to Stand*, in addition to multiple rewrites, fragments, and corrections over a period of approximately two years. There are at least three drafts of *Some Problems for the Moose Lodge*, the one-act that is the germ for the full-length play, dated May, September, and November of 1980. This was followed by *The Dancie Money*, composed in late 1980 and early 1981, dated "Jan. 1981." There are two other 1981 drafts, both titled *A House Not Meant to Stand*. The first dates to January and February of that year, and the second of these was performed at the Goodman Studio Theatre in April of 1981 and is labeled "The Post Studio Goodman Version." The latter was revised in a draft dated "February 1982." The final draft of *A House Not Meant to Stand* contains some elements of all the earlier drafts, but it was extensively streamlined and much of it was rewritten. Most of what was cut involved specific political statements and monologues by Cornelius, as well as almost all jokes about Bella's weight. A retyped version of the final, 1982 script was later distributed by Williams' agent at the time, International Creative Management [ICM], a copy of which was sent to New Directions. While some of these drafts are available in archives at Harvard and Columbia, copies of all the major drafts, unless otherwise noted, are housed in the Special Collections of the Chicago Public Library, Goodman Theatre Archive.

The text for this edition is taken from Joseph Drummond's stage-manager script used for the final Goodman Theatre production that opened on April 27, 1982. It includes many details, especially entrance, exit, and sound and light cues, and an entire page, which were missing from the ICM script. All stage directions have been conformed to Williams' style, and the opening stage directions have been slightly augmented to incorporate aspects of the final production which Williams discussed with the designers, director, and producers, but did not have the opportunity to rewrite for publication. Part of Williams' initial description of the set—beginning with "The curtain rises upon . . ." and ending with ". . .extravagance of 'see-through.'" —is taken from draft notes for this play in the Columbia University Library. The epigraph and notes quoted in the Introduction come from that same fragment, at the top of which is written, in Williams' hand, "Projected next version," below which is typed, "Being Addressed by a Fool." The description of Bella in a fragment titled "Our Lady of Pascagoola" is from the Harvard University Library archives.

The set designed for the Goodman Theatre production in 1982 by Karen Schulz showed the fragility of the McCorkle house using moveable, opaque scrims for many of the walls. Depending upon how the scrims were lit, they could appear to be solid walls or be seen through, disappear completely to reveal other rooms or a longer view of the staircase, or even, as shown in the frontispiece photograph, reveal an upstairs room with a crib and children's toys. This design choice also helped to focus in on other areas of the stage when it was necessary, and to separate the dining area for Bella. These scrims were combined with lighting and sound effects to add to the continual motion of the scenes and the sense of precariousness in the McCorkle house: thunder, lightning, traffic sounds, dripping, creaking, power failure, and the cries of children playing.

A special souvenir program published for the occasion by the Goodman Theatre provides a helpful description of the set design:

> "To evoke the simultaneous reality and illusion of *A House Not Meant to Stand*, designer Karen Schulz has devised a selectively realistic interior whose skeletal framework (comprised of steel tubing and realistic doors, stairs, and railings) defines walls which instantly "melt away" to suggest the changing psychological perceptions of the main characters. To achieve this, wall units are covered with scrim, a loosely woven material which becomes transparent when lit from behind. Walls are painted with a series of exaggerated designs, heightening the feeling of unreality which pervades the play. The entire setting is placed on a series of raked platforms skewed towards downstage left, thus emphasizing the off-center world of the McCorkle home. The setting is extended upstage through the use of an elevated platform, giving added height and depth to the playing area."

Williams meant for the dialogue of the spectral children—as well as that of the apparition of Chips which shows Bella where the money is hidden—to be prerecorded and heard through a sound system in the theater. In the original Goodman production, the child actor who played the "young Chips" at the end of the play also performed as the ghostly apparition of Chips in the earlier scene. In a production of *A House Not Meant to*

Stand produced at the Southern Repertory Theater in 2004 by the Tennessee Williams/New Orleans Literary Festival, the challenge of the apparitions was handled somewhat differently. In New Orleans, they cast three children, plus an adult to play the apparition of Chips. The latter choice allowed for a "real" ghost by visually projecting the idea that the recently deceased Chips has come back to help his mother. The actors cast as the adult Chips and the three children filmed their respective scenes on the set, without the other actors, so that the footage could be projected during performance onto the scrim in front of the dining-room area. In this way, the shouts and dialogue of the spectral children were heard from all around the theater and then, on film, they appeared to be with Bella, and later sitting right with her at the table, holding hands together while they all said grace. This was very effective and probably solved other problems involved with child actors entering and exiting the scenes, and staying up late.

As has been noted in the Introduction, Cornelius was the name of Williams' father, Cornelius Coffin Williams. It seems Williams did even more picking from the family tree when considering character names for *A House Not Meant to Stand*. C.C. Williams had two sisters, Isabel and Ella, whose names combine to make Bella. It is also worth noting that the maiden name of the character Bella Dancie McCorkle is not a far stretch from the maiden name of Williams' own mother, Edwina Estelle Dakin. According to the Williams family tree prepared by Richard F. Leavitt and Allean Hale for the Norton paperback edition of *Tom: The Unknown Tennessee Williams* by Lyle Leverich, Williams' paternal grandmother was the daughter of Francis McCorkle whose wife, Isabel Sevier, was a direct descendent of the famous Valentine Sevier (nephew of Jesuit missionary Saint Francis Xavier), after whom the character of Valentine Xavier was named in *Battle of Angels* and *Orpheus Descending*.

EDITOR'S ACKNOWLEDGMENTS

I first approached Gregory Mosher about my interest in *A House Not Meant to Stand* in the spring of 2001, and he has been supportive, discerning, and immensely encouraging ever since—and as a bonus, he is a superb storyteller. I would like to thank Gregory for his contribution to this volume, and point out, as he would not, that his patience and his faith in Williams are in fair measure responsible for the author's completion of this play.

The staff of the Goodman Theatre was responsive and friendly about any question I had for them, there were many, and they supplied enough research material that it arrived in two good-sized boxes. My gratitude goes to Roche Schulfer, Managing Director, Robert Falls, Artistic Director, Steve Scott, Amber Hilgenkamp, and Erin Moore, as well as to Sarah Welshman of the Chicago Public Library. Members of the original production staff, stage manager Joseph Drummond and set designer Karen Schulz Gropman, kindly went over aspects of the 1982 production and their input has helped to make the text of this edition accurate. Karen Gropman also loaned me her file on *House* that contains photographs, programs, and reviews. Members of the original cast, Scott Jaeck, who played Charlie in all three productions, and Cynthia Baker who played Stacey, conveyed memories of their experiences and what it was like to work with Tennessee Williams. So did Peg Murray who shared her reflections on playing the role of Bella at the Goodman, and also her love of Williams, her passion for his genius, and her memories of creating roles in three of his plays.

Doyenne of Williams scholars, Allean Hale, has been expectedly generous and gracious, lending me first reading copies of *Some Problems for the Moose Lodge* and *The Dancie Money*, answering various questions, and sharing her considered opinions. I am also grateful to Williams scholars Nicholas Moschovakis, Annette J.

Saddik and John S. Bak who have been helpful with insights, questions, and moral support, and to Williams scholar Philip C. Kolin who invited me to write a chapter on this play for his volume, *The Undiscovered Country, The Later Plays of Tennessee Williams.* I have been fortunate to work with others from the community of Williams scholars over many years, and I am grateful for their input and exchanges, formal and informal, on this and many other projects: Jack Barbera, Robert Bray, George Crandell, Colby Kullman, Al Devlin, Kenneth Holditch, the late Lyle Leverich, Brenda Murphy, Michael Paller, Barton Palmer, Brian Parker, David Roessel, Nancy Tischler, and Ralph Voss.

This is an opportunity to thank those who have been generous with their time and expertise on a variety of Williams-related projects, and I am happy to acknowledge Tom Erhardt and Georges Borchardt, theatrical and literary agents, respectively, for the University of the South, heirs to the Estate of Tennessee Williams who graciously authorized this publication; my friend Paul J. Willis, Patricia Brady, Elizabeth Barron, Doug Brantley, among many others from the Tennessee Williams/New Orleans Literary Festival; Mark Cave, Curator of Tennessee Williams Manuscripts at the Historic New Orleans Collection; Genie Guerard, Head of the Manuscripts Division at the UCLA Library, Department of Special Collections; Richard Workman, Research Librarian at the Harry Ransom Humanities Research Center, University of Texas at Austin; the late Richard Freeman Leavitt, the late Eve Adamson, Michael Raines, David Kaplan, Jeremy Lawrence, John Uecker, Scott Kenan, Panny Mayfield, David Landon, Randy Gener, Fred Todd, Pamela Beatrice, Jef Hall-Flavin, Andreas Brown, Michael Kahn, Donna Pierce, Margaret Bradham Thornton, Dan Isaac, William Jay Smith, David Cuthbert, Edward Albee, Anne Jackson, Eli Wallach, John Guare, Lanford Wilson, John Lahr, John Waters, Rodrigo Corral, Sylvia Frezzollini Severance, Griselda Ohannessian, and Peter Glassgold. On a more personal note I want to thank Barbara Epler, Declan Spring and all my colleagues at New Directions, as well as Nancy Keith, and Arturo Noguera.

My deepest gratitude goes to New Directions president and publisher, Peggy L. Fox, who worked closely with Tennessee Williams and from 1977 has been his primary editor. Since 1988 Peggy has allowed me to contribute in small and large ways to the publication of Tennessee Williams' works by New Directions, and ten years ago she entrusted me with editing this volume. I am indebted to Peggy for her confidence and friendship.

Five Plays. NDP506.
In Search of Duende.† NDP858.
Selected Poems.† NDP1010.
Nathaniel Mackey, *Splay Anthem*. NDP1032.
Xavier de Maistre,*Voyage Around My Room*. NDP791.
Stéphane Mallarmé, *Mallarmé in Prose*. NDP904.
Selected Poetry and Prose.† NDP529.
A Tomb for Anatole. NDP1014.
Oscar Mandel, *The Book of Elaborations*. NDP643.
Abby Mann, *Judgment at Nuremberg*. NDP950.
Javier Marías, *All Souls*. NDP905.
A Heart So White. NDP937.
Tomorrow in the Battle Think On Me. NDP923.
Your Face Tomorrow. NDP1081.
Written Lives. NDP1068.
Carole Maso, *The Art Lover*. NDP1040.
Enrique Vila-Matas, *Bartleby & Co*. NDP1063.
Montano's Malady. NDP1064.
Bernadette Mayer, *A Bernadette Mayer Reader*. NDP739.
Michael McClure, *Rain Mirror*. NDP887.
Carson McCullers, *The Member of the Wedding*. NDP1038.
Thomas Merton, *Bread in the Wilderness*. NDP840.
Gandhi on Non-Violence. NDP1090.
New Seeds of Contemplation. NDP1091
Thoughts on the East. NDP802.
Henri Michaux, *Ideograms in China*. NDP929.
Selected Writings.† NDP263.
Dunya Mikhail, *The War Works Hard*. NDP1006.
Henry Miller, *The Air-Conditioned Nightmare*. NDP587.
The Henry Miller Reader. NDP269.
Into the Heart of Life. NDP728.
Yukio Mishima, *Confessions of a Mask*. NDP253.
Death in Midsummer. NDP215.
Frédéric Mistral, *The Memoirs*. NDP632.
Teru Miyamoto, *Kinshu: Autumn Brocade*. NDP1055.
Eugenio Montale, *Selected Poems*.† NDP193.
Paul Morand, *Fancy Goods* (tr. by Ezra Pound). NDP567.
Vladimir Nabokov, *Laughter in the Dark*. NDP1045.
The Real Life of Sebastian Knight. NDP432.
Pablo Neruda, *The Captain's Verses*.† NDP991.
Love Poems. NDP1094.
Residence on Earth.† NDP992.
Spain in Our Hearts. NDP1025.
New Directions Anthol. Classical Chinese Poetry. NDP1001.
Robert Nichols, *Arrival*. NDP437.
Griselda Ohannessian, *Once: As It Was*. NDP1054.
Charles Olson, *Selected Writings*. NDP231.
Toby Olson, *Human Nature*. NDP897.
George Oppen, *Selected Poems*. NDP970.
Wilfred Owen, *Collected Poems*. NDP210.
José Pacheco, *Battles in the Desert*. NDP637.
Michael Palmer, *The Company of Moths*. NDP1003.
The Promises of Glass. NDP922.
Nicanor Parra, *Antipoems: New and Selected*. NDP603.
Boris Pasternak, *Safe Conduct*. NDP77.
Kenneth Patchen, *Collected Poems*. NDP284.
Memoirs of a Shy Pornographer. NDP879.
Octavio Paz, *The Collected Poems*.† NDP719.
Sunstone.† NDP735.
A Tale of Two Gardens: Poems from India. NDP841.
Victor Pelevin, *Omon Ra*. NDP851.
A Werewolf Problem in Central Russia. NDP959.
Saint-John Perse, *Selected Poems*.† NDP547.
Po Chü-i, *The Selected Poems*. NDP880.
Ezra Pound, *ABC of Reading*. NDP89.
The Cantos. NDP824.
Confucius to Cummings. NDP126.
A Draft of XXX Cantos. NDP690.
Personae. NDP697.
The Pisan Cantos. NDP977.
The Spirit of Romance. NDP1028.
Caradog Prichard, *One Moonlit Night*. NDP835.
Qian Zhongshu, *Fortress Besieged*. NDP966.
Raymond Queneau, *The Blue Flowers*. NDP595.
Exercises in Style. NDP513.
Gregory Rabassa, *If This Be Treason*. NDP1044.
Mary de Rachewiltz, *Ezra Pound, Father and Teacher*. NDP1029.
Margaret Randall, *Part of the Solution*. NDP350.
Raja Rao, *Kanthapura*. NDP224.
Herbert Read, *The Green Child*. NDP208.
Kenneth Rexroth, *100 Poems from the Chinese*. NDP192.
Selected Poems. NDP581.
Rainer Maria Rilke, *Poems from the Book of Hours*.† NDP408.
Possibility of Being. NDP436.
Where Silence Reigns. NDP464.
Arthur Rimbaud, *Illuminations*.† NDP56.
A Season in Hell & The Drunken Boat.† NDP97.
Edouard Roditi, *The Delights of Turkey*. NDP487.
Jerome Rothenberg, *Pre-faces & Other Writings*. NDP511.
Triptych. NDP1077.
Ralf Rothmann, *Knife Edge*. NDP744.
Nayantara Sahgal, *Mistaken Identity*. NDP742.
Ihara Saikaku, *The Life of an Amorous Woman*. NDP270.
St. John of the Cross, *The Poems of St. John* ... † NDP341.
William Saroyan, *The Daring Young Man* ... NDP852.
Jean-Paul Sartre, *Baudelaire*. NDP233.
Nausea. NDP1073.
The Wall (Intimacy). NDP272.
Delmore Schwartz, *In Dreams Begin Responsibilities*. NDP454.
Screeno: Stories and Poems. NDP985.
Peter Dale Scott, *Coming to Jakarta*. NDP672.
W.G. Sebald, *The Emigrants*. NDP853.
The Rings of Saturn. NDP881.
Vertigo. NDP925.
Aharon Shabtai, *J'Accuse*. NDP957.
Hasan Shah, *The Dancing Girl*. NDP777.
Merchant-Prince Shattan, *Manimekhalaï*. NDP674.
Kazuko Shiraishi, *Let Those Who Appear*. NDP940.
C.H. Sisson, *Selected Poems*. NDP826.
Stevie Smith, *Collected Poems*. NDP562.
Novel on Yellow Paper. NDP778.
Gary Snyder, *Look Out*. NDP949.
The Real Work: Interviews & Talks. NDP499.
Turtle Island. NDP306.
Gustaf Sobin, *Breaths' Burials*. NDP781.
Voyaging Portraits. NFP651.
Muriel Spark, *All the Stories of Muriel Spark*. NDP933.
The Ghost Stories of Muriel Spark. NDP963.
Loitering With Intent. NDP918.
Symposium. NDP1053.
Enid Starkie, *Arthur Rimbaud*. NDP254.
Stendhal, *Three Italian Chronicles*. NDP704.
Richard Swartz, *A House in Istria*. NDP1078.
Antonio Tabucchi, *It's Getting Later All the Time*. NDP1042.
Pereira Declares. NDP848.
Requiem: A Hallucination. NDP944.
Nathaniel Tarn, *Lyrics for the Bride of God*. NDP391.
Yoko Tawada, *Facing the Bridge*. NDP1079.
Where Europe Begins. NDP1079.
Emma Tennant, *Strangers: A Family Romance*. NDP960.
Terrestrial Intelligence: International Fiction Now . NDP1034.
Dylan Thomas, *A Child's Christmas in Wales*. NDP1096
Selected Poems 1934-1952. NDP958.
Tian Wen: A Chinese Book of Origins.† NDP624.
Uwe Timm, *The Invention of Curried Sausage*. NDP854.
Morenga. NDP1016.
Charles Tomlinson, *Selected Poems*. NDP855.
Federico Tozzi, *Love in Vain*. NDP921.
Tomas Tranströmer, *The Great Enigma*. NDP1050.
Yuko Tsushima, *The Shooting Gallery*. NDP846.
Leonid Tsypkin, *Summer in Baden-Baden*. NDP962.
Tu Fu, *The Selected Poems*. NDP675.
Niccolò Tucci, *The Rain Came Last*. NDP688.
Frederic Tuten, *Adventures of Mao on Long March*. NDP1022.
Dubravka Ugrešić, *The Museum of Unconditional Surrender*. NDP932.
Paul Valéry, *Selected Writings*.† NDP184.
Luis F. Verissimo, *Borges & the Eternal Orangutans*. NDP1012.
Elio Vittorini, *Conversations in Sicily*. NDP907.
Rosmarie Waldrop, *Blindsight*. NDP971.
Curves to the Apple. NDP1046.
Robert Walser, *The Assistant*. NDP1071.
Robert Penn Warren, *At Heaven's Gate*. NDP588.
Wang Wei, *The Selected Poems*. NDP1041.
Eliot Weinberger, *An Elemental Thing*. NDP1072.
What Happened Here. NDP1020.
Nathanael West, *Miss Lonelyhearts*. NDP125.
Paul West, *A Fifth of November*. NDP1002.
Tennessee Williams, *The Glass Menagerie*. NDP874.
Memoirs. NDP1048.
Mister Paradise and Other One Act Plays. NDP1007.
Selected Letters: Volumes I & II. NDP951 & NDP1083.
A Streetcar Named Desire. NDP998.
William Carlos Williams, *Asphodel* ... NDP794.
Collected Poems: Volumes I & II. NDP730 & NDP731.
In the American Grain. NDP53.
Paterson: Revised Edition. NDP806.
Wisdom Books:
The Wisdom of St. Francis. NDP477.
The Wisdom of the Taoists. NDP509.
The Wisdom of the Zen Masters. NDP415.
World Beat: International Poetry Now From New Directions. NDP1033.

For a complete listing request a free catalog from New Directions, 80 Eighth Avenue New York, NY 10011; or visit our website, www.ndpublishing.com

†Bilingual